EDGES
Of
EXISTENCE

EDGES
Of
EXISTENCE

3 Shorter Works

James I. McGovern

Copyright © 2012 by James I. McGovern.

Library of Congress Control Number: 2012904590
ISBN: Hardcover   978-1-4691-8052-6
             Softcover   978-1-4691-8051-9
             Ebook   978-1-4691-8053-3

All rights reserved. No part of this book may be reproduced or transmitted in any form or by any means, electronic or mechanical, including photocopying, recording, or by any information storage and retrieval system, without permission in writing from the copyright owner.

This is a work of fiction. Names, characters, places and incidents either are the product of the author's imagination or are used fictitiously, and any resemblance to any actual persons, living or dead, events, or locales is entirely coincidental.

This book was printed in the United States of America.

To order additional copies of this book, contact:
Xlibris Corporation
1-888-795-4274
www.Xlibris.com
Orders@Xlibris.com
113515

CONTENTS

The Case of Arlene—9

The Lightweight—55

The Celestial Opera—125

To Gerry, brother and good enough guy

THE CASE OF ARLENE

1

Jobs were scarce during the recession, especially for someone my age. I was lucky enough to land a part-time spot at a rural mental health facility. As a counseling aide, I would mostly visit and talk casually with a list of residents. This gave the real professionals some relief, though it was theoretically for the benefit of the residents. If I heard anything significant I was to inform my supervisor, Lucerna. She and I were outside one day, discussing my list, when we noticed a female resident staring at us. The woman was short with wild gray hair, a small pale face with sharp features, and she had a wiry build.

"She looks excited," Lucerna remarked. "Unusual for her."

"You're back!" the woman called over. "Back!"

"Yes," I said loud enough to carry. "Every Monday, Wednesday, and Friday."

The woman smiled, appearing delirious.

"That's Arlene Doe," said Lucerna. "We already had a Joan Doe and Joanna Doe in our files when she came. We named her Jolene Doe but she didn't like it. 'Make it *AR*lene!' she said. So we did."

"You gonna talk to me?" Arlene asked.

"He's just leaving," said Lucerna. "Maybe next time."

We turned to go.

"*Will* you?" Arlene demanded. "*Really?*"

I looked to Lucerna, who nodded.

"Sure!" I called back, and we continued walking.

"What about the gender thing?" I asked.

All the residents on my list were male, in accordance with policy. Arlene was no doubt on the list of a female counseling aide.

"We'll get an exception," Lucerna answered. "Nobody's been able to get anywhere with her. I'll give one of your other cases to Harry. Or, I can assign Arlene to myself but you do the talking. Either way it's for her benefit. She's been like a clam in here."

"Okay," I said. "Glad to help."

Lucerna gave an amused smile, perhaps thinking *that's what you're here for*. She was about ten years younger than me, a confident professional.

We continued into the building, I holding the door.

That was the first day.

2

Case Name: Doe, Arlene

Throughout our conversations, many of client's supposed memories are fragmentary and quite muddled. Little can be understood from them. Her earliest account with any coherence concerns walking down a street to buy a magazine.

As she walked, an occasional gust of wind would blow her hair back from her face. Arlene would raise her shoulders then and shudder within her coat. The old houses seemed to be ignoring her. They were sullen, drained of their color under the stormy sky. The red ones seemed the saddest. Now and then, a leaf would flutter down in front of her. Why were they falling in spring? The trees were so scraggly, like they were sick. Still, they were something. Without them just narrow old houses pushing right up to the street.

She came to a corner drugstore. She'd bought popsicles here when she was little but they didn't sell them anymore. She entered and went to the magazine rack. The owner, an old man, used to get mad when kids would stand here reading the comic books.

"Do you have the June *Seventeen*?" she asked him.

"Not in yet. Should be in a couple days."

A bright cover caught her eye and she saw that it was *Time*. "The Hippie Phenomenon." Picking the magazine up, she found that the article was long. She'd have to buy it.

Outside, she tucked the magazine under her arm and walked down the business street. Small storefronts were soaped or papered over on the inside, *For Lease* signs taped against the glass. A small food store was closing for the day, the owner pulling a metal grate across the front, putting a padlock on.

Coming to another corner, she shielded her eyes from a whirl of dust. There was distant thunder and the county jail sprawled before her. Crossing over, she walked along the fence, gazing in at the massive structure. The wind played with her hair, making her squint with its gusts. There were prisoners inside, people locked up for doing something wrong, maybe hurting someone. But if they wanted to escape, was that wrong? It was if they meant to hurt someone, but just wanting to escape, by itself—who could blame them?

A car was honking across the street, a boy she knew asking if she wanted a ride. Arlene shouted back, saying she'd walk, and the car sped off. Then she must have gone home.

A separate memory found her in her bedroom, reading for school. The clock ticked loudly and her eyes would stray once in a while to the other bed in the room. Its spread was white with little tufts and there was a pennant on the wall over it. Her sister was away at college, but it would only be for a year. Money was short.

Shouts came from the living room. Pa was watching the ball game with her brother and another guy. They were drinking beer.

Laying her book aside, she sat up on her bed.

It had been fun here once. That was when she was little, playing around the neighborhood and getting into trouble. But high school had been hard for her, and Ma and Pa watched her so close. Her brother, too. It was the movies or dance and come right home. That was the whole date. She might as well be going with another girl.

She got up to brush her hair. A friend of hers, another girl, was coming over soon. Arlene had nice hair then, light brown with gold highlights, a little curly. She'd always been fair to pale, with hazy blue eyes. She sat straight as she brushed, petite but strong.

More shouts from the living room.

She found her friend in the kitchen talking to Ma, who had her worried little look. If only Arlene could convince her that everything was all right, nothing bad was going to happen. They were just going for sodas and maybe to the other girl's house. Why was Ma so worried, looking up like that as she sewed up the holes in their socks?

"What time will you be in?"

"By ten, Ma, I think."

"Be careful now."

"Sure, Ma."

There was a screen door that slammed and wooden steps on which their feet must have been noisy. Here the memory faded.

3

Case Name: Doe, Arlene

Client recalled a job she had in a dungeon-like factory, cartons of paperback books piled up to the ceiling. This was the warehouse she walked through on her way to the bindery. Other women in green work dresses moved slowly ahead of her, mostly in twos or threes. There were men too, laughing and swearing. Sometimes one of the huge brown bugs that lived in the cartons would run out into the aisle. Arlene had thought they were mice at first.

She would stand on the line with seven or eight other women, a supply of book sections behind her. She would turn around, take a section from each pile, put them in order, turn around, and stuff the unbound book into the metal conveyor-rack. Then she'd do another one, and another and another, for eight hours not including lunch. When she was next to "A.B.," the friendliest of the other women, it wasn't so bad. They would talk together and the shift would go by faster.

"When you going back to school, honey?"

"Just about a month, A.B."

"Think you'll miss this place?"

"I don't know. Maybe a little."

"No, you won't. You're too smart for that. Even I am. Even *I'm* too smart to like working at *this* place."

"Oh, A.B. I meant the people. You and a couple others."

"Sure wish *I* could go back to school. But I'm too old. Too old to go sitting in a classroom."

"No, you're not. There's lots of people *older* than you. They have special classes for adults and all."

"Hm. School's not what I need nohow."

"Oh? What is it you need?"

"A rich old man who'll marry me then die. That's what *I* need!"

"A.B.!"

"That's right, honey. Someone I can just bury and have all his money so I won't ever be poor again."

They'd go on and on this way, packing book sections all the time. A.B. would occasionally ask Arlene if she were ready for a break.

"I'm always ready."

"So am I. Too bad we have to wait for that man to turn the line off. He might as well go around with a whip, the way he works us."

"The men just walk off when they want."

"Mm. You're learning, honey."

Eventually, they'd touch on Arlene's boyfriend, A.B. nodding toward a male coworker who grated on her.

"Your boyfriend's not like *that—is* he, honey?"

"Oh, no. He's nice."

"I hope so. But you got to be careful, honey. This here is a man's world. Don't you forget it."

Perhaps the coworker's emphasis helped strengthen this much in client's memory. No further details came through, however, about the job or her other life at the time.

4

"I'm impressed," said Lucerna. "What's your secret?"

We were at a table in the staff lounge, Lucerna smoking.

"I can't say. She hits on something, I act interested. She says what she says."

"Good enough technique."

She tipped an ash from her cigarette, looking down at the metal ashtray. I noticed a concentration in her, a stillness to her sallow features, her loosely bunched brown hair.

"Have you thought about taking courses, Tom? Adding some credentials? If you have a knack—well, maybe there's a future here for you."

I laughed but caught myself. She was serious, after all.

"I'm kind of far along for that."

She looked at me a moment, then shrugged.

"You never know."

She blew some smoke toward the vending machines, dismissing the subject.

"Now the boyfriend, she sort of skipped over him. Right? It'd be nice to know some more on that. Maybe you can steer her back that way."

"She's kind of rough steerage."

"Steerage. I haven't heard that word for a while. Well, if anyone can steer her, you can. I'm glad I put you on her."

I felt a bit awkward and couldn't respond at first. After all, I was only there to make a few bucks till something better came up.

"I'll do all I can," I managed.

A woman came in to tap the coffee urn, cheerily greeting us on the way. Lucerna gave a distracted wave.

"I wonder," she said. "Maybe I should pull another case from you. Or two, even. I want you to give Arlene plenty of time."

5

Case Name: Doe, Arlene

Something with the boyfriend had happened during the summer, something nice Arlene thought, and it affected her when she was back in school. The other girls, their activities, seemed too silly to her, as if they didn't know what was important, which was someone like Rick, or Nick, or maybe it was Rico or Stan. (To be called Rick in this narrative.) The school subjects, some of them at least, seemed more important to Arlene since she needed them for college, for her and Rick's future.

He was in junior college but took little interest in his courses, it turned out. When Arlene asked what subjects he was taking, he'd have trouble remembering. Their sole purpose was to keep him safe from the draft. He spent a lot of time at the campus, however, and much of his remaining time at work, pumping gas. Arlene saw him less than ever.

"Rick," she said, "what do you do all the time at the campus?"

"Hang out. The lounge, the cafeteria, the gym."

"Who do you hang around with?"

"Guys from my classes. Friends. Whoever's around."

Guys. Always the guys. But inside, he wanted to be with her like during the summer. She was sure of it. He'd talked about a night at a motel, some time he wasn't pumping gas. It was okay that he didn't care about school, just so he cared about *her*. But what about the future? He didn't seem to care at all about that.

"Rick, do you think we might get married?"

"Huh?"

"If we keep going like we are now, do you think it'll end up that we get married?"

His response was to blow smoke hard and double up in laughter. When he was spent, he took a deep breath and laughed all the harder.

"Rick, don't."

She took his arm and squeezed it, but he couldn't control himself. That night, Arlene went to bed rather puzzled.

Later, she apparently pressed for an explanation.

"Look," he said, "I like you. I like you a lot. But I don't go with you 'cause I want to marry you. Christ, why should I get married? I don't like kids, I don't have a good job—hell!"

"We could still get married if we want."

"But baby, I don't want to."

"Why do you go with me, then?"

"Like I say, I like you and—well, I figure I should put in some time with you."

"What? Put in *time* with me?"

"Yeah."

"What do you mean? Why *put in time*?"

"'Cause we been doing it."

Within herself, Arlene began to hate the man—his appearance, his talk, his emotional distance. She suddenly hated everything about him. School was what counted now. Not all the silliness that went on, but the things that were interesting and made her think. It was important, of course, to have someone like Rick, to have a man. But his attitude and the hassle from her parents were too much. As winter set in, Arlene would study hard and put Rick off when he called. She saw a girl friend when she wanted company, though she realized it would never be good enough with another woman.

Client recalled another walk on her street, wondering why people didn't shovel their snow. The sidewalk was icy from packed down snow after many had walked on it. When it was windy then, or dark, it was easy to fall down.

There was no moon this night, only dim, dirty streetlights. The snow was all dirty and crusty, the flat-faced stone houses looking frigid, adamant: You are not welcome. There was no one on the streets, the cold keeping them in. Too cold for robbers and jerks, Arlene thought. Stay in and keep warm, make trouble when it's nice out. More lights ahead, the business street. Why am I out here walking? The cold, the pain of winter—feels good when you go in. Light at the end of the tunnel. All emptiness now but, somehow, there's hope.

She passed an old lady holding a shawl over her head, shivering, picking her way along the ice.

She was like me once. Time and weather, the cold. And hard work and sadness. Life isn't just hard. It can be brutal to some people. A conscious, deliberate force that hits them again and again until they submit, until they are broken. And when they are miserable, they just stay that way. Until they die and everybody forgets about them.

She passed a tavern that was still open. The beer smell came through even though the tavern was shut tight against the cold. County Jail was across the street, also shut tight.

Oh, that wind! So freezing in the darkness, so much worse than when there's light. Sweeping down from the Arctic, across Canada. Is winter nicer in the country? It always looks so nice on Christmas cards.

Arlene became silent but was smiling, perhaps dwelling on inexpressible thoughts.

6

A miniature fountain trickled on Lucerna's desk, filling the gaps in my reporting on my clients. Neither of us liked to meet in her office, I because it gave a bad feel from my past, being called on the carpet in other places. She had reports to finish for the administrator, though, so we hadn't much choice today.

"Harry was good about another transfer from you," Lucerna commented. "Josie bristled a little with hers, got into the gender policy and all. But we'd already crossed that line when I gave you Arlene. And she's a priority now, pure and simple."

"It's all okay with Mrs. Arnold?" I asked, referring to the administrator.

Lucerna kept her eyes on her papers.

"So far, so good," she answered.

I saw my supervisor as efficient, methodically clinical, but with some kind of underlying impatience. She had a distaste for mundane details and would skip over them if she could get away with it. This tendency could propel her further into testing limits.

"Actually, I'd like to let a student handle those cases, but there's those state guidelines. Paid staff only, accountability."

She spoke with something like sarcasm. Clearly enough, she chafed under restraints even while working diligently. I felt some desire to help her.

"Maybe you could have a student help with your reports," I suggested. "That would free you up for other things."

She looked up with a surprised smile.

"Confidentiality, Tom. But thanks for your sympathy."

The little fountain trickled close to where I sat. It was the only noise for a moment as I returned her look, the new feeling beneath our formal roles. She shared the quiet office with another supervisor who wasn't there but could return at any time.

"You know," Lucerna said, "with the complications in Arlene's story, we might do better to discuss her off-campus. Give it our undistracted attention. Next time, maybe, if that's all right with you."

"Sure, I'd be happy to."

"Good."

We got back to work then, but I had the sense we'd moved to a new phase in relation to each other, something beyond our obligations to Arlene and others at the facility. Yet Arlene was the catalyst. Or rather her case was, her condition. If this went anywhere with Lucerna and me, we'd more or less owe it to Arlene.

7

Case Name: Doe, Arlene

Client has had memories of attending college, or rather, scenes and incidents of that period in her life. She apparently commuted to an urban campus. Of the college itself, she recalled sitting in an outdoor amphitheater, other students also sitting or sprawled on the stone steps. Autumn sun was flooding in, creating a glare, but her sunglasses protected her.

"Che! Che! Che!"

A dozen or so demonstrators with signs marched into the space below. Students looked up non-committally from their books or conversations.

"Che Guevara lives forever in the collective conscience of the masses!"

The leader's words reverberated over the stone steps and his companions cheered. Arlene watched them, detached, recalling a news photo of the slain revolutionary. Finality, she thought, there's no denying it. Dead is dead.

Arlene enjoyed being in college. She'd always sit near the front of the lecture hall since people were talking and fooling around farther back. When there was a test, she had no trouble applying herself to studying. When she was only reading or preparing a written assignment, however, her mind would often wander.

Almost every day she found herself idling somewhere on the campus. She'd sit in one of the cafeterias, or in a lounge, or somewhere outside, and read or pretend to read or simply do nothing. She was waiting, really. Not for someone from one of her classes. They would simply talk about the class. Nor for someone she'd known in high school. She was waiting for someone new, someone who was interesting and fun and would introduce her to people and activities that would make her life full and important. She'd taken up smoking and felt secure and sophisticated as she sat and waited amidst the fading wisps of her cigarette.

Sometimes, rather than simply idle, Arlene found little activities to attend. She took in the experimental films that were shown for free, sitting by herself in the dark of the viewing room. Few people attended these films except for one which showed hippies copulating in a pig sty. Arlene also went to hear the guest speakers, many of whom were radical. She only had to pay once, when Dr. Leary came. The huge room was packed as he spoke against the war and antagonists of the drug culture. His wife sat beside him holding a huge flower, and it occurred to Arlene that this woman was only a few years older than she.

It was easy to know what there was to do. Bulletin boards were everywhere, announcements seeming to fight each other for space. Arlene would often examine them, even in the rain, as other students hurried by. By the end of the quarter, she was very curious about the short, strongly-worded messages from the SDS and other groups of radicals.

Client recalled an incident from a job she held during Christmas season, apparently during that first year of college. It was behind a counter at a downtown department store. Her feet would hurt after a few hours and she'd be bored and restless. She'd watch the shoppers rushing along, eager to spend money, and think of the dollar thirty-five an hour she was being paid. It somehow didn't make sense to her, didn't seem fair. The experience was uninteresting and painful and the rewards for her pain weren't enough. Things just didn't balance out.

"Do you have this in a fuchsia?"

"What?"

The older woman smiled in condescension.

"Fuchsia, my dear. It's a color—light, bright reddish purple."

"Let me check."

Arlene opened the cabinet below the counter and brought out some cashmere sweaters.

"We don't seem to have one in exactly that color. Here's one in a rose color. Is that close enough?"

"No, my dear, I'm afraid not. Rose is simply not fuchsia. Here, let me see those."

Arlene watched the aged hands picking through the sweaters, the delicate gold watch with little diamonds, the rings with stones that just couldn't be real, she thought.

"Tell me, what do you charge for seconds in this item?"

"All our seconds are sold at half price."

The shopper pulled a light blue sweater out of the stack.

"Here. Look at this."

"What?"

"Can't you see? This sweater is soiled."

"It is? Where?"

"Look. See, right here."

The woman waved her finger toward the neckline. Arlene looked closely but couldn't see what the woman was talking about.

"I'm afraid I don't see anything. Maybe it's the light."

"Nonsense. This sweater is soiled and should be sold as a second."

Arlene hesitated. What was this old lady trying to do?

"No, ma'am. The price is $39.95."

"I insist you sell it to me at half price!"

"No, ma'am. I can't do that."

"You'll do it or I'll see the manager and have you fired!"

Some people looked over and a wave of embarrassment warmed Arlene. What a bitch this woman was! Why didn't she just wipe herself with it? Then it would really be dirty!

"Well, are you going to ring it up?"

Arlene laughed in her face.

"What! We'll see about this!"

She flung the sweater back and bustled off, shooting back grimaces. Arlene refolded the sweater and put it away with the others. Thinking on what had happened, she didn't feel bad. She'd been spontaneous, yet she'd been right. Cut through the complications, she thought, like the radicals at school. They're right sometimes but they act kind of crazy so people don't listen.

The holiday season was windy and snowless and Arlene was eager to get back to school. The decorations reminded her of her job in the department store, and she didn't feel as close to her family as before. She felt lonely on New Year's Eve, wishing she was in a snow-covered cabin, snuggled close to someone in front of the fireplace. Someone strong, gentle, intelligent. Someone who had ideas like a radical but was respected by people and not aggressive.

With the winter quarter came snow and bitter cold. Jeeps were plowing snow all over the campus, and the central amphitheater was just a big white bowl with an icy path through its center. Over this path students rushed from the library to the Student Union and vice versa.

Once in a while, since she couldn't sit outside, Arlene would sit in the Student Union's TV rooms, where a set in each room was continuously tuned to a single station. She'd still check all the bulletin boards, though, for things more interesting. One afternoon, when it was already getting dark, she saw a young man in hooded jacket tacking up announcements. It was very cold but he seemed unhurried as he tapped with a small hammer. Passing behind him, Arlene stopped to view the announcement. The young man turned and smiled at her.

"It's a McCarthy rally. They'll be organizing volunteers for the Wisconsin primary."

Arlene took a half-step sideways, about to walk on, but there was something in his easy movements, his speech, and his eyes that she couldn't walk away from.

"Will there be peace movement speakers?"

"Sure, people from lots of different groups. McCarthy's campaign manager will be there to handle the recruitment."

"Will you be there?"

What made her say that? Before she could become embarrassed, however, the young man smiled and put her at ease.

"Of course. Why don't you come? I'll introduce you to some of the peace movement people if you like."

"Okay." And she smiled back at him.

Although his hood was up, she could see his hair was dark blond and longish. Some fell over his forehead and more stuck out along the sides. She couldn't see what color his eyes were; they were set deep and the sun had gone down.

"By the way, my name is Jim."

Although he might have said Tim, Arlene thinks now, or even Jack. But we decided to stay with Jim for our conversations.

"I'm Arlene."

"You look cold."

"Yes. Guess I'll go to the Union and warm up."

He said he'd see her later, at the Union or at the rally. Arlene isn't sure which it was, just that it seemed colder than ever when she was away from him.

8

"You're getting a lot from her," Lucerna commented. "A pretty decent history. And interesting. I can sense the period."

We were in her apartment, close to the facility but beyond its control. We sat on opposite ends of a couch, tubular steel and black leather. There were abstract paintings on the walls, as well as primitive masks, and carved wooden figures of animals on tables and shelves.

"She can really come out with the details once she gets going," I said.

Lucerna nodded over the folder, cigarette in hand.

"So now we have Jim, not Rick. Rick's out of the picture."

"So it seems. For now, anyway."

"Yeah, we don't know where she's going to take us. She doesn't either, I suppose. We don't know how much of this even happened. Right?"

I nodded my assent.

"I was wondering," I ventured, "if we were going to involve Dr. Greenberg soon."

The facility was occasionally visited by a consulting psychiatrist, our state's budget not permitting one on the permanent staff.

"No," Lucerna said absently, "later." She studied the folder. "This is a little before my time, but—" A coy smile. "Not yours, right?"

"Yep, I'm about that vintage."

Her smile widened.

"But a little sweeter variety, I'd say."

I was stuck for a response. She was my supervisor. Yet, curled on the couch without a therapist coat, she looked quite appealing for early middle age.

"Actually, I have some around. You've given me a taste now. Have a glass with me? No guarantees, but I sort of like it."

"Well, I have the drive."

I was living in another town, traveling to and from the facility past rural plains. But Lucerna just kept looking at me, waiting for me to say more.

"I guess just one would be okay."

She flipped on the sound system on her way to the kitchen. Subdued band music floated through the living room. I looked toward the patio door, the failing light outside. I considered switching on a lamp, but Lucerna was returning already with glasses of wine.

"So," she said, "you're really into Arlene's life. It's amazing after all the months of stonewalling we got."

I shrugged.

"I'm as surprised as you are."

"And you never did this before, got someone to open up like this, as a counselor of some sort?"

"Not really. I was just a case manager—financial, medical, making referrals to people like you who knew what they were doing."

She held up two fingers crossed.

"Let's hope so."

"Well, I mean probably."

"Yes, probability. Good as anything to live by. Right?"

"I suppose."

She'd made no move to put on a light, was sitting a cushion closer to me on the couch. I sipped my wine, leaving the ball in her court. Experience dictates discretion.

"Want to dance?" she asked.

What else could I do? I lowered my glass to the coffee table as she drank deeply from hers. She led me to an area before the patio door lit by the remnants of sunset. The band played on from the sound system hidden in shadows.

9

Case Name: Doe, Arlene

It might have been after the rally, or maybe another time, but client recalled walking through slush with Jim and another male, Jim's friend. They were talking about whether or not to attend a certain concert. They reached Jim's car and he dropped off the friend, then turned to Arlene sitting beside him.

"Like to stop by the Monk's Cell?"

"What's that?"

"My apartment."

"Why do you call it a monk's cell?"

"Because it's very small," he smiled, "and very humble."

They drove only a few minutes and then turned into a quiet side street where Jim parked. Arlene followed him to a two-story cottage behind an old stone house. They climbed an outside staircase to the second floor, where Arlene waited as Jim searched for a light switch inside.

"Does anyone live downstairs?" She asked.

"Yes, a restaurant worker. Nice guy."

The room was lit by a dim, unshaded bulb. There was an old stove next to a sink and a large metal box, painted black.

"What's that?" Arlene asked.

"My refrigerator."

"Why is it black?"

"I don't know. It was like that when I moved in."

The apartment was just one big room with a sort of bathroom closet added. There was a mattress on the floor and an old, scarred desk with a lamp on it. Books and art materials were scattered about and there were masks and posters on the walls. Jim gestured toward cushions on the floor and Arlene sat down.

"Like some fruit juice? I have tea, but I know you drink coffee."

"What kind of juice is it?"

"Kumquat."

"Are you serious?"

He poured two small glasses from a pitcher in the black refrigerator. Handing one to Arlene, he sat in front of her and proposed a toast.

"To peace."

"Yes, to peace."

They drank.

"Are you really a radical?" Arlene asked.

He looked to one side and seemed to concentrate. When they were in quiet, dimly lit places, his eyes appeared so deep beneath his mane of hair that Arlene saw him as a lion.

"In my political beliefs, in my attitude toward society, I guess I am. But in my personal values, my ideas on a lifestyle, there are probably a lot of people who feel the same way and don't seem radical at all. I'm basically a very simple man, Arlene."

He hesitated a moment, then continued.

"I feel the need to support radical causes, to work actively for them, because we live in the shadow of tyranny. It's the same in other countries. As long as the present pattern exists, this state of everyone being at the mercy of a few politicians, generals, and millionaires, there has to be some resistance. Otherwise, it means we accept their total power, no matter how unfair or arbitrary their decisions."

"Do you think the radicals can win?"

"In our country, probably not. It doesn't seem possible. But we can influence the power brokers' decisions on individual issues. Like right now there's the war."

"I like the way you describe things, Jim. It makes me understand them better."

"Thanks, but I don't really have any answers. I can only support movements that seem to be in the right direction."

Arlene glanced around the room.

"How long have you been living on your own?" she asked.

"A couple years. Since high school. I moved in here in the fall."

"It must be nice—not having anyone to answer to, just coming and going as you please. And you can study without any distractions. I like the way you live. You're so free!"

Jim smiled and leaned toward her.

"Yes. But you know, Arlene, quite often I feel lonely. So I tend to go out a lot."

"It's funny, Jim. I like to go out, too, but not because I'm lonely. It's more to get away from the people at home. I don't feel free with them. I feel closed in. I feel like I'm being forced to live their way, to believe what they believe."

"Most parents, I think, will only treat their children as adults after they have children of their own."

"But that's not right."

"No. But it isn't important, either."

She studied his face, his confident smile, and felt a decision rising.

"I like you, Jim. I like you a lot."

"I like you too, Arlene."

She toyed with the small glass that had held her kumquat juice, waiting out the emotion that was rippling through her. Jim studied her hand, her blue eyes, her brown and gold hair, curly near the ends.

"Want to stay?"

Arlene nodded.

She awoke in the Monk's Cell next morning as winter sunlight filtered through the room. Against her heart she held Jim's sleeping head and twined his tawny hair around her fingers. She could feel the warmth of his body in the chill morning, and the warmth of her own.

This was peace.

10

The bedroom was dark except for outside light filtering in. It was brighter than it would usually be due to fresh snowfall, still in progress. Lucerna lay beside me, turned away on her side, breathing quietly. I myself hadn't slept yet. She'd wanted to dance again on this visit, but this time it led to something more, a lot more. The wine, our growing familiarity, and that certain anxiety in her, that need, opened the way to here, her bed.

Looking at her dim form, I wondered where this might lead. What was possible for us? Like me, Lucerna apparently had a rocky past in her relationships, though I didn't have many details on them.

"He flipped out," she'd said of her ex-husband.

"What do you mean? How?"

"That's *it*. He just flipped out."

There was also the place we worked, the facility. Anything between staff members was noticed, talked about, and Lucerna was my supervisor. The administrator, Mrs. Arnold, had a friendly, folksy way about her, but I was wary of an underlying rigidity so common in these semi-rural areas. She wouldn't be administrator if she didn't share in it.

I leaned over to touch Lucerna's shoulder.

"I'm awake," she said.

"I guess I am, too. Not dreaming, I mean."

She turned over so she faced me, raising herself on an elbow.

"Having second thoughts?" she asked.

"About what?"

She laughed.

"Maybe you're thinking about another go-around."

"Well, the snow's pretty deep by now, I think."

She relaxed back onto the pillow.

"Yes, we have all night."

"Actually," I said, "I was thinking about you. How you might have been early on, just out of school and getting into your chosen work."

"Hm, yes. Full of enthusiasm, professional zeal. Then, not too far along—"

"Hit a wall? Disappointment?"

"More like stagnation, with an occasional sense of purposelessness."

"But, the humanitarian thing, helping people. Isn't that what drove you, starting out?"

"Ah, those telltale words, 'starting out.' Before you know how entrenched everything is—the institutions, attitudes, financial and legal stuff, et cetera, et cetera. And knowing that, in the end, you're not going to make a damn bit of difference for the parade of pathetic creatures who come in. Knowing you're just part of the official BS."

I hesitated. I'd had this conversation before. Other times, other places.

"A crappy system, yeah. Most systems are. But if it's all you have to work with, what can you do? Just your best, right? And no regrets."

"You believe that, Tom?"

"Well, I'm able to. It's an available response."

She was silent for a moment.

"Would you like to move in here?" she asked. And when I didn't respond, "It'd be handy for snowstorms."

We both laughed.

"There's that difference that's there," I said, "between visits and all the time. A good relationship can get ruined. Maybe inevitably."

"Speaking from experience?"

"Yes. Though things can go wrong in many other ways, too."

"How true. But then, if it wasn't we wouldn't have much business."

And we wouldn't have met, I thought—wouldn't be meeting here to discuss a special case. I reached over to touch her and she caught my hand, pulled me toward her. The sound of a passing snowplow marked the end of our conversation.

11

Case Name: Doe, Arlene

Client recalled that, through the placement office at college, she'd gotten a summer job as a day camp counselor. There were jobs that paid more, but factories and stores and such were part of her past now. She was escaping from the treadmill.

As a counselor, she'd take the children places or teach them things and feel as important to them as a mother. She could be firm when necessary and was pleased when a child responded to her correction. But her main satisfaction was that, for a few hours a day for a few months, these children needed her. Her meeting their needs added meaning to her existence.

"Jim," she said, "I think I want to major in something where I can work with people. Helping them, I mean. I like the feeling it gives me."

"Well, there's teaching, social work. Nursing, too, but that takes a lot of science."

"How about if I major in psychology?"

"Yeah, you could be a counselor, social worker, something like that. Maybe pretty high-paying if you go to grad school."

She looked at him in the dim light of the Monk's Cell. Sounds of the city at night could be heard through the open windows.

"You don't really care about all that—do you, Jim?"

"About all what?"

"Grad school, careers, and all."

"Well, no, I guess not. Working with people is something different, though. I might get into it myself, in some way."

She lay back and looked at him. He'd been unusually quiet this night.

"What do you think about when you're so quiet?"

"Oh, sad thoughts mostly. About time, how hard it is to hang on to something good, once you find it."

"Do you have something good now?"

He leaned over and kissed her.

"So do I, Jim. But don't ever think about losing it."

"I can't help it, Arlene. I got a letter from the draft board today. They reclassified me."

"Took away your deferment?"

"Right. Oh, I won't get drafted tomorrow. Sooner or later, though—"

They were silent a moment.

"Will you go, Jim?"

"No, of course not."

She took him in her arms and laid her head on his chest.

"Let's not worry about it tonight. Maybe you can just get it changed."

He laughed slightly and caressed her hair.

"Okay, no more of that tonight."

※

Client's memories of the convention riots were fragmentary and disordered, difficult to elucidate. She was apparently living away from her family at the time, presumably with Jim. Many activists were pouring in from out of town. They camped in a large park area, living a freewheeling lifestyle. Their plans for the convention were often preparations for conflict, and there were preliminary skirmishes with police. There was much drug abuse, arrests, rising anger and resentment of authority.

There was a march downtown, where the radicals were to join with more moderate groups and march on the convention center. There was conflict with police along the way, with much shouting and defiance, objects thrown, beatings, tear gas, running and regrouping. Most of the radicals, Arlene and her friends among them, reached the point of convergence with the other demonstrators. On trying to approach the convention, however, they were confronted by phalanxes of blue-helmeted police.

Arlene recalled a voice on a bullhorn, a token warning perhaps, and blue lights flashing everywhere. Then the police charged in with Mace and flailing clubs. The beating went on and on, Arlene scrambling to get away past fallen bodies. There was a chant that rose from the periphery, a chant that the world was watching. Then all went blank.

Sometime after the convention, Arlene and Jim walked through drizzle near a city train station. He looked straight ahead as he walked, she down at the sidewalk, at the cracks.

"I want to go with you," she said.

"It wouldn't be good just now. I have to find a place and get myself together. And you need to stay in school."

"I need to be with you, Jim. Don't you see?"

He bit his lip and heaved one of his knapsacks into a more secure position.

"Yeah, I see."

She looked at him as they stood at the last stoplight before the train station. So good and great he was, yet pushed around and beaten by slobs, hate-filled weaklings. Now he was forced into exile because he wouldn't do their dirty work, their killing and blowing up. Forced away from his friends and places he knew, forced away from her, and she from him.

"I'm sorry, Jim. I'm making it harder for you. You're right, of course. I should stay in school and go later. We'll live together just like we did here. Won't we?"

"Sure. Of course."

They entered the huge station and took an escalator down to the old waiting room with its massive benches. She stood with him as he waited to buy his ticket.

"Damn it, Arlene. I'm sorry."

"No, that's all right. I'll be okay."

He kissed her.

"I'll write and call you, and you'll be coming up later."

They forced smiles and hugged each other.

"I like that, Jim. I'll think about it all the time."

But she cried in the departure area, thinking again about the unfairness of it all. She collapsed into his arms and sobbed against his coat. It was always this way, she thought. As soon as you found something good—happiness or a way to help people—complications set in and suffocated, strangled, shut off the life—the promise—of all that you had. The world seemed just one big bureaucracy controlled by ruthless, invisible sadists.

"Stay with Zoe for a while. She's a really good person."

(He might have said Zoila or something else, client's memory of names again an issue.)

She didn't reply but stopped sobbing. She could feel his heart beating.

"I have to go now, Arlene. The train leaves in a few minutes."

They kissed and he picked up his bags. Out on the concrete pier, they embraced again as he boarded the train. Then he swung his knapsacks up and leaned over from the steps.

"Good-bye, and peace."

"Yes, peace."

And they kissed for the last time.

12

Case Name: Doe, Arlene

Client recalled studying a great deal, letting her mind be stimulated and new curiosity fill the void left by Jim's departure. She wanted to absorb what she studied and become more, grow intellectually. She believed there was power to be gained from knowledge, power that would enable her to control her own life, achieve what she needed. She sought to escape forever the swamp of mediocrity that had held her captive.

The very language of psychology, Arlene's major, came to attract her. She enjoyed thinking of behavior in terms of motivation and levels of consciousness, or personality in terms of hereditary versus environmental factors. She'd build up her knowledge of psychology and deepen her understanding of people until they could no longer hurt her.

Besides the knowledge, there was the simple thrill of functioning intellectually. Her mind was becoming tuned, exercised, so it could make correct decisions based on her growing store of knowledge. She was no longer just her physical self. She was a mind, someone whose opinions were informed, who could converse with other intellectuals on important matters. It was partly because of Jim and partly because he left her. Because, after he left, she had to study so much to escape the pain.

"Are you awake?" asked Zoe. "You got a letter from Jim."

Arlene looked up at her roommate from where she lay on the couch. Zoe was taller than herself and dark-haired.

"Thanks."

She took the envelope and examined the familiar handwriting, the Canadian stamp and postmark. Within herself she felt a stirring, something prodding her to be curious and troubled. She opened the envelope and read the letter.

"What's he say?"

"He got a job working on a loading dock. Still living with those two other guys, moving out soon. Nothing much else."

"Mm-hm. So, will you visit him soon?"

"Yeah, I guess so. After he moves."

Their eyes met.

"Sorry I woke you."

"No, that's okay."

"Are you still tired?"

"Yes. Think I'll go to bed early."

They shared a large double bed and had to pile it with quilts and blankets since the heat went off at night. At first, Arlene thought of herself as sleeping alone, accustomed as she was to her life with Jim. But as time went by and the winter grew colder, she began to feel safer and cozier in the knowledge that her strong and loyal friend was lying next to her.

"Arlene?" Zoe spoke in the dark.

"Mm-hm?"

"Are your sheets warm yet?"

"Almost. Why?"

A hesitation.

"There's kind of a draft over here. Can I come closer?"

"Okay."

There was no anxiety, no regretting later what happened. And they did it again. Within the darkened city apartment, a connection was achieved, an intimate sisterhood that dispelled all thoughts of the world outside.

※

As she sat on the western side of the library, looking up from her books toward the declining sun, it occurred to Arlene that everything was because of Jim. He'd made her see the importance of being educated, developing intellectually. And it was through him that she'd met Zoe, whom she now loved even more than she loved him. Now, while she could reject him without guilt—reject him as a man, reject his love—she could never reject what he represented. His lion's mane, she believed, covered a mind that was refined in a way that would be central to her own development, her own success. This was something that Zoe seemed to understand and yet didn't identify with herself. And Arlene didn't wish to convert her, pressure her into accepting the rigors of intellectual development. The acceptance of each other as they were was vital to their relationship. Nonetheless, she became increasingly aware that Zoe was a creature of the physical world whose wisdom was rooted in something other than intelligence.

One day near the end of summer, as Arlene was walking through a chilly drizzle, the answer to everything came very suddenly. She was on the edge of the city, in an upscale neighborhood on the lake, and she shivered within her jacket. She'd been feeling stressed and used some pills that Zoe had, but they sometimes had bad effects. She needed something else. As she looked up at the sky, gray but not dark, it suddenly seemed that there was great meaning. Everything was as it should be and good because things were as they were by the hand of Someone or Something greater than everybody. She felt such an abundance of meaning and human goodness in her that it lit the entire street, gave it life.

There was a church in the distance. Arlene felt drawn to it.

As she approached, she noticed a door propped open and many cars parked outside. It was Sunday morning. Standing before the sign, she read the denomination, different from her own. No matter; a church was a church. They all seemed holy.

Once inside, she hesitated. The minister was standing at a podium in front, reading a report of some kind. An old man sitting on the aisle turned around and scrutinized her. A younger man sitting next to him pulled on his arm and urged him to pay attention. Pushing back her damp hair, Arlene stepped forward. Ignoring the congregation, she walked directly toward the front of the church and the minister. He stopped speaking as she drew near, returning her gaze in silence until she halted in front of him.

"Good morning, sister. The usher will show you to a seat."

A man approached from one side but, before he could take Arlene's arm, she dropped to her knees.

"Behold the handmaid of the Lord!"

Minister and usher looked at each other dumbly, then back at Arlene.

"Behold the handmaid of the Lord!"

Her cry mesmerized all present. She was holding out her arms in supplication. The usher was powerless but the minister recovered and beckoned to his wife in the front row. She got up and came forward.

"I'm the mother of God!" Arlene shouted. "I'm having your baby! Your spirit is filling me and bursting out! Light of the world! I'm the holy virgin!"

"Hallelujah!" someone shouted. It was the old man. "She's saved! Hallelujah!"

He was jumping up and down, people trying to restrain him. At the front, the minister's wife talked cajolingly to Arlene.

"Sister, come with me. Pastor will talk to you after the service. Come with me, now. I want to help you. Come."

Arlene looked at her blankly, then struck out with a clawed hand and left four red streaks across the woman's face.

"Shut up with your crap! I'm the light of the world!"

"Hallelujah!" the old man shouted. "Praise God she's saved!"

The minister came from behind the podium and stood in front of Arlene. She looked at him and spoke imploringly.

"I'm the mother of God! I'm having your baby! Take me into your house and make love to me!"

The minister's wife was sobbing on the floor, holding the wounds on her face. The usher, totally confused, looked desperately to the minister.

"Get the police," he was told.

13

The restaurant had plenty of candles but not much other light. Lucerna and I had held off ordering dinner, wanting to talk awhile over cocktails. She was tenser than usual, smoking, gazing into open spaces of the restaurant. Mrs. Arnold was across the room with her husband and another couple, well into their meal. Lucerna had acknowledged her superior with a brief wave but otherwise avoided eye contact. Her only comment on the situation had been "Oh, no!" when she first noticed it. I'd taken a quick glance.

"We'll have to bring Greenberg in on Arlene," Lucerna said.

"It's gone that far?"

"Yeah, you're into his territory. Then there's her." A head jerk toward Mrs. Arnold. "She'll be reading the file now."

"She'll involve herself with the case?"

"I hope not. Not too much, anyway. We want it to cover *this*, with us."

I nodded along but sensed a problem developing.

"Look, if a change becomes needed, I'm just part-time. I can find something else. There's no need for you to have to deal with it."

Lucerna frowned, flicked ash from her cigarette.

"No, no change. We have Arlene's case. For that bitch over there that's all this is."

"Right," I responded, refraining from further suggestions. Like Lucerna, I really didn't want any kind of change for us.

"Guess it's good you didn't move in," she said. "They'd have us dead to rights."

I laughed. Lucerna didn't.

"I'll get copies of your reports to Greenberg," she continued, "arrange a meeting on Arlene for his next visit."

"Any way I can help?"

"Just talk with Arlene, then have the new material ready for the meeting." A hesitation. "I mean, if you were asking professionally."

I glanced again toward Mrs. Arnold.

"Guess that's all I better do here."

43

Lucerna finally smiled.

"They'll be leaving before us. Then we'll do what we want, *where* we want."

"Consenting adults."

"Of sound mind."

The restaurant patter continued around us. We eventually had dinner, then drove past rural plains to my place in another town. The thought of Mrs. Arnold's scrutiny kept us from Lucerna's this night.

14

Case Name: Doe, Arlene

Client had little recall of the period following her breakdown, but she apparently resumed her studies and managed to graduate, eventually finding employment as a school counselor in a rural community. She rented a room on the edge of town and bought an old used car to drive to work. She liked her job and people respected her, but there was something very wrong for her. When she came home to the big house full of rented rooms, there was nothing there for her, no one who cared about her professional status. She was intensely alone in the long quiet nights. She didn't want a relationship, afraid from the past of what might happen, but there was still that gnawing need within her. Of necessity, then, her work came to be everything for her. She *was* her work. She'd be defensive if anyone disagreed with her because they threatened her existence.

The last student she counseled, who might have been named Randy, had been suspended for misconduct on the school bus. Another boy had written a word on Randy's hand and given him a nickel to show the word to the bus driver.

"Do you know what that word means?" Arlene asked.

"No, ma'am. If I knew it was a bad word, I wouldn't have done it. Honest."

She looked at the suspension notice: extremely immoral behavior, indefinite suspension. It was signed by the grade school principal, recalled as "Mr. Smetters."

"How long do I have to stay home, ma'am? I'm not too good at arithmetic and I might flunk if I miss too much."

"I don't know, Randy. I have to talk with your parents and get back to Mr. Smetters. We'll get you back soon as we can. Okay?"

She smiled but Randy didn't. He was worried, didn't want to flunk.

"Are we friends, Randy?"

"Yes, ma'am."

The parents were quite passive, Arlene found, submissive to the will of the school. She was thus alone in her efforts to persuade the principal. Her previous contacts with him had been brief and formal, no real issues having arisen during her month or two on the job.

"Mr. Smetters, I think that Randy should return to school tomorrow, that his suspension should be lifted."

"You do, Arlene?"

"Yes, sir." She explained about Randy's fear of falling behind, her plan to work with the family, the other boy's setting Randy up.

"Yes," the principal responded, "I know that's what he says."

"He's really sorry for what happened," Arlene went on, "and of course we don't want his education to suffer."

Mr. Smetters leaned back in his chair and swivelled slowly to one side.

"So the boy likes school, eh? Perhaps, then, the best guidance for him is to keep his suspension in effect."

Arlene couldn't speak for a moment.

"I don't understand, sir. What do you mean?"

He swivelled back, fixed her with his eyes.

"You say the boy is sorry and wants to return to school, that you and the parents will be working with him. Fine. But the question in *my* mind is this: Has he learned?"

Arlene was silent.

"When I say 'learned,' I'm not talking about anything we can teach him in a classroom—arithmetic and such. I'm talking about something more important, *far* more important. I'm talking about moral values."

He went on then about moral correction in the young, how small infractions eventually grew into violent and despicable acts. Morally inferior children grew into morally inferior adults with no sense of responsibility. Their beloved community would deteriorate. When he stopped talking, Arlene struggled to think as she made one last entreaty.

"Sir, is there some other way he could be punished? You see, I feel responsibility toward *both* things: his personal development—the morals and all—and his education. I wonder if we can't help the one without hurting the other."

The principal hesitated, his expression blank, then again swivelled away.

"Maybe. I'll let you know."

She learned of his decision the following morning as she sat in her office at the high school. The phone rang and one of Randy's teachers, sounding upset, asked her to come to the grade school right away.

"Why? What's the matter?"

"The principal is having a public slapping! Of Randy!"

"What?"

"He's assembling the entire school. Then he's going to stand up on the stage and slap Randy's face. His parents agreed to it. It's the only way he can get back in school."

"You must be joking. Aren't you?"

"No, Arlene, I'm not. And Mr. Smetters says he's doing it on *your* advice!"

Feeling suddenly dizzy, Arlene hung up and rested her head in her arms. As the dizziness passed, a familiar anger swirled up from somewhere below her heart, gathering at her temples and heating her.

The auditorium was full by the time she arrived. There were a good many adults as well as the children. Randy sat in a chair on the stage, sidelong to the audience, and his parents were seated behind him, sharing in his guilt. Mr. Smetters stood before the boy, removing Randy's glasses, handing them to a teacher who stepped back to give the principal room.

Whap!

Randy's face was twisted toward the audience and Mr. Smetters was reaching back to deliver a second blow.

"Stop it, you bastard!"

Arlene ran up to the stage and stood below the principal.

"You son of a bitch! Slapping little boys! Go to hell with your stupid, self-righteous morality! All he wants is to get back in school, but you have to make a *spectacle* of him, show off your sick, perverted *authority*! Your need for power, to compensate for everything you lack as a *person*!"

Mr. Smetters leaned away from her, shaken. Everyone else in the place was frozen and silent. Randy watched her through his tears, but he too was unmoving.

"You talk so much about morality," Arlene continued, "then you do something like this! You're just covering up your urge for power—wanting to see people suffer while *you* control them! You *bastard*!"

The principal's arms hung limply at his sides. He looked out confusedly over the audience. Arlene turned and met a multitude of shocked expressions, a sea of bewilderment and fear. They didn't understand. Why was she shouting obscenities in their school? Maybe she was crazy. A counselor but crazy herself.

The nearest exit was on one side of the stage. Arlene ran for it and no one made an effort to stop her.

15

We were in the conference room at our facility, Lucerna and myself facing Dr. Greenberg across the table. He was engrossed in the new report I'd brought. A plate of brownies, brought in by Mrs. Arnold, sat conspicuously before us. Dr. Greenberg had enthusiastically tried one but then neglected it as my report absorbed his interest. He was middle-aged, heavy for a doctor, and wore thick glasses below his curly hair.

"Well—" he intoned as the report dropped from his hands. His expression was one of enlightenment, but solemn. He hesitated, making a steeple of his hands, then continued.

"Lot of pain in this woman, deep down, been there forever. Almost." He gave me a friendly look. "Great job by the way, eliciting so much."

I gave a slight shrug.

"But the pain," he went on, "always there, the fear of more. The fear. Well. I'll have to see her, no question. Not today, but block off next time—the whole period. Or, if you can swing a special appointment—"

Lucerna gave a disconsolate look.

"Good one, doctor. The budget? Block off a session, okay, as long as Mrs. Arnold—"

"I'll talk to her myself. This is important, vital. The duration of suffering here, the long-standing lack of therapy, should give it the highest priority."

"It's strange how she fell through the cracks," said Lucerna. "You'd think that somewhere along the line, with all the contacts she must have had, someone would have gotten her treatment. People should have picked up on it, should have helped her."

Greenberg removed his glasses, studied them as he responded.

"It speaks to the sad state of public services. Those most in need can drift for years, decades, floating on the fringe of society. Testimony to our low ebb of humanitarianism."

He put his glasses back on and squinted at me.

"It's amazing how she opened up to you, after we'd had so little success. *No* success. There must have been some key, something that unlocked her to you."

"Tom's modest about his success," said Lucerna.

"I don't mean a technique or skill necessarily—no offense, Tom—but a circumstance of some sort, a chance factor, a quirk. As if you remind her of someone or something exempt from her resistance, so she can open the album of her past to you."

"It's not always very clear," I said, "and there are many periods blank. Not to mention her entire later life."

"Those decades of apparent wandering," said Lucerna.

Greenberg appeared thoughtful.

"Perhaps that time can be investigated. I have my contacts in the courts. We'd want to establish the veracity of what she's given us, anyway."

I listened carefully, trying to picture what might be down the road. What material had I provided, I wondered, that might lead to Arlene's identification?

"Well," said Lucerna, "it seems we're making real progress. I feel optimistic. And proud of you, Tom. It's your work that finally put things on track for Arlene."

"No question about it," Greenberg added, reaching for his unfinished brownie.

I smiled modestly.

"And in case I forget," he said looking at Lucerna, "please let her know that I found these delicious."

Wry smiles were exchanged as the psychiatrist nibbled.

16

Case Name: Doe, Arlene

Client described at length her long drive northward to see Jim. She took expressways at first, but then she was on smaller roads, gliding past dormant forests and struggling farms abandoned to winter. Occasionally there were snowflakes in the air and she'd think of the holiday seasons she'd known and the nicer ones that she'd imagined. And yet continually she'd found herself in sullen, oppressive places, alone and uninspired. Nobody seemed to care anymore about the delicate, the beautiful, the true and fair.

There was someone, though, who would never put her down, who'd given her the spark of life and would renew her now when she needed him again. He'd been confused when she called, but he must have been happy too because he said all right come. There was another who might be there but somehow they'd get some time together and he'd speak to her in the soft, strong tones of many seasons ago.

As she neared the city, industrial sheds and metallic junk gradually replaced the gray farms and blackened forests. She wasn't sure how to find the address, so she stopped at a gas station for new directions. The man was friendly and told her to enjoy her stay in the city. It made her feel good, more confident that she was doing the right thing. The happiest time of her life had been those few months with Jim, and she hadn't even realized it. She hadn't seen the absurdity of trying to improve on perfection.

It was growing dark by the time she found his building. The snowflakes were blowing in gusts over the pavement, where leaves and paper were scattered also. She locked her car and struggled against the wind up to Jim's building. The inner door was unlocked and the stairs very quiet, as if waiting for her to tread them. She knew which door was his but the thought of backing down presented itself on the dark, smooth surface before her. When it faded for a moment, she knocked quickly before it could return.

"Oh. You made it."

"Hi, Jim."

"Come on in."

He'd put on weight, especially around his stomach, and his hair was cut short. It was darker than she remembered it, and his eyes were lighter, or maybe shallower.

"What are you doing these days?" he asked.

"Well, I had a job in community mental health, but I just left it."

There was a woman coming in from the kitchen.

"This is my wife, Marie."

His *wife*? She had dark hair, long and wavy, but seemed a little overweight. She was wearing an apron and had her hands in the pockets. She smiled but it was a courtesy smile, like the light inside a car.

"Would you like a beer?"

"Uh, no. Thanks"

"How about you, Jim?"

"Sure, I'll have one."

"Coffee, Arlene?"

"No, nothing. Nothing for me."

Marie left the room, clearly at ease and maybe amused, Arlene thought. She acted as if she owned the place. But then, here was Jim now married to her. Arlene wondered what had happened to the philosophy, the poetry of his life.

"Are you still an activist?" she blurted.

He was startled, then something like embarrassed.

"Uh, I go bowling sometimes. But aside from that, I'm either at work or with Marie."

There was a moment of silence. Jim laughed slightly to break it and, for a fleeting instant, Arlene saw the man she'd known in the Monk's Cell.

"It's been a long time," he said. "We're different people now."

There was a sound then that she couldn't believe she was hearing, on this night and at this place. Marie was striding quickly into the room as the noise continued. She set down two cans of beer and then quickly retreated.

"You'll have to excuse me. Eric's awake."

Jim was smiling as he watched Marie go. Arlene looked down, waiting for his fascination to pass. The air felt like gelatin around her.

"How old is he?"

"Going on three months."

It was gone: everything he had been and hoped to be. He was a different man now. The past was irretrievable.

"I'm starting computer school in January. Nights, of course. We'll be moving when Eric gets older and I'll need a better job."

"What were you doing now, Jim? What *are* you, I mean."

"Still driving the forklift. Thought I could hook on as a mechanic, but it didn't work out. Somebody's friend got the job."

"They're talking about amnesty back home."

"I know."

"Do you think you'd go back?"

He hesitated, looked down in thought.

"There's a lot of things to consider."

Marie brought out the baby and gave him to Arlene to hold. Staying for dinner was suggested, and watching something on TV, but Arlene felt a desperate need to leave. Jim offered to walk her to her car, but Arlene said no. She wanted only to escape. The wind had eased outside and a thin layer of snow had covered the neighborhood. She ignored her tears as she brushed the snow off her car, then off her coat. She didn't look back at the window of their apartment, even as she pulled away, fiddling with the heater instead. She'd seen Jim for the final time when she'd turned to descend the stairs.

Until quite recently.

17

It was the middle of the night. We were in Lucerna's bed, she breathing steadily in sleep. Minimal light came through from outside, allowing me to sense forms as I lay awake, reflecting on our expired evening.

We'd had dinner at a Chinese buffet, making the trips back and forth and amusing each other with our selections. It was in a mall, so later we browsed past indoor store windows, avoiding the raw wind outside. Lucerna stopped before a display of engagement sets, but we moved on with vague smiles. She showed more spirit before a luggage offering.

"Why don't we take a vacation, Tom?"

"Where would you like to go?"

"I don't know, someplace warm."

"Warm would be nice."

"Though *you're* good with the cold, too. Maybe you like it better."

"I could always handle it pretty well."

We went on to a store with funny clothing, then to a book store we decided to enter, our banter growing slightly more serious. Later, in the car, Lucerna relaxed with her head back, eyes closed, while I drove to her apartment. We were becoming close, I saw, in more subtle ways now. Quiet understandings were developing.

Now, in her bed, I sensed the empty wine glasses out in the living room, the CD still in the machine though the music had run its course. We were in post-intimacy, a time for sleeping though only one of us was doing so.

I was more awake than I'd been all night, actually. I was thinking of my last report on Arlene, mailed so it would reach Lucerna this coming work day. I wouldn't be at the facility when she read it. I didn't plan on going there ever again. My last talk with Arlene had exhausted my capacity to illuminate her past. It was up to Greenberg now to fill in the gaps, to assign meanings and suggest a plan. For me the road ahead was a mystery, as it always had been since Marie grew distant, remaining herself really while I, Tom/Tim/Jim, reverted painfully to my college persona.

"Don't you realize those times are over?" she'd demanded. "Gone forever!"

"I'm not *trying* to slide back," I'd said. "It just comes to me by itself."

I had to walk around, quietly slipped out of the covers. Lucerna wouldn't be surprised, I knew, if she woke and found me gone. I hadn't always stayed the night, what with Mrs. Arnold's scrutiny. And Lucerna was well accustomed to being alone in bed.

Eric was a man himself now, solid, working in business under better mentors than me. Marie had remarried after the divorce, her spouse a no-nonsense contractor.

I passed the coffee table where I knew the wine glasses stood, taking care to not upset them. I thought of the CD still in the machine, recalling the music we'd enjoyed, but left the disk where it was to avoid making noise. I dressed in the dark. Arlene's visit may have started things, I thought, brought me eventually to this room, this secret exit from a lover, a job, and a former lover. But maybe it would've happened anyway, memories and sentiment driving me to ramble until I found her, set things right in some way, helped her if only a little. I couldn't undo what had happened to her, couldn't have prevented it in the first place. But maybe I'd changed her direction, her downward spiral, so that others more competent than me could help her salvage something from life.

I found my coat, looked around in the dark, said goodbye in my mind to Lucerna. I slipped out the door as quietly as I could. I pulled away in my car.

I'd ramble on, I knew, with my own issues unresolved as ever. My efforts with Arlene had been for my benefit as much as hers: to lend value to my existence, some affirmation. But the forces around me and those deep within were, as always, too great for my actions to make a difference. I had never been truly romantic, yet never a good realist. I wasn't quite a schizoid, but was basically unreachable, in my own personal limbo. And the worst—or maybe best—part of it was that I liked it.

I drove on into the night.

THE LIGHTWEIGHT

1

A name, but with an explosion the name of a death,
one of the countless in the stirrings of a war.
But then, the next year, the name reborn,
a baby on a blanket on a wide green lawn.
Smiling, unaware of his smiles,
the baby looks out at flowing dresses and baggy pants,
the women watching under big curls,
the men with grimness as they sip their drinks.
The baby doesn't know why he's watched.
He only knows life
and wonders.

2

Toddling through the post-war economy,
the early frost of the Cold War,
the little boy discovers dandelions,
yellow then gray puffs of seed,
shaken or blown through his universe.
He blinks at the sun, watches rain from a window,
puzzles over storms in the night,
but then the milkman is there in his white suit and hat,
trading milk for their clean empty bottles.

3

The person he's always around, his mother,
skirt swishing, grabs him and pulls him along
to lunch, or long rides on a streetcar,
sparks showering over people in hats.
They visit other women, two with silvery hair,
another with a girl who walks wobbly.
At night comes the form of his father, dark coat with business hat.
Later the boy feels hair tousled, turns to see
his father's smiling profile passing,
medicine smell coming from tinkly glass.
His father sits dimmed amid musty cigar smoke,
cooking sounds coming from the kitchen.

4

Television, new to adults as to the boy,
pulls his stare into wooden cabinet,
the black and white world within, puppet shows
and the talking giraffe who wants a Clark bar.
The boy smiles, hearing the giraffe talk to him,
and wants a Clark bar too, for himself.
But then Friday Night Fights and Jackie Gleason,
other shows too that flow past him,
he sitting on the floor,
his questions too many to ask, to interrupt.
There's the crowning of Elizabeth, reminding
the boy of church, and the McCarthy hearings.
An angry witness rises to leave, followed by
the taunts of the man in charge:
"You're running away! You're running away!"
The boy laughs, finally understanding them,
but his mother, watching tensely, shushes him.

5

Growing up, the boy learns to print, make numbers,
straight and tall with a pencil, soft paper, blue lines.
Then he writes, making loops, adds the numbers, subtracts.
He learns the sounds of letters, reads out loud.
It sounds choppy. But he does it, never questioning.
The question forms in church, amid clouds of incense,
the magical sacrament that requires belief,
fast and abstinence, confessing of sins.
He doesn't see the magic but it doesn't bother him.
It must be there since the others all believe:
his extended family with parties in their basements,
laundry tubs full of beer and ice,
all doubts awash in laughter and song—
who is he to interfere?
Back at school they have air raid drills,
hiding under desks from pretend bomber planes.
He doesn't see why Russia would bomb their school,
doesn't question but doesn't worry either.
He treats it as he does the magic sacrament.

6

Just once, an unreal summer, he goes to camp,
active boys in barracks with religious men,
men without women.
There's the usual, expected things,
the boats, swimming, ball playing,
but the boy excels in fringe activities,
knocks someone down in boxing,
loses only to a counselor in the long race.
He's restless like the others during crafts,
but feels pride with his hinged wooden box,
bird's head burnt into lid, varnished over.
He gets top award at the end, though first in nothing,
perhaps because, in his innocence and fire,
the religious men see themselves,
claim him as their own.

7

Heavy bundles dumped on the steps overnight,
taken to the basement where he rolls as shown,
clumsy at first then easier with time, repetition.
The bulging sack too much on his bike
so he walks, carefully placing a *Herald*
by each designated door,
stale weekly news from the factory-class suburbs.
When he does his collections he counts money slowly,
stacking half-dollars in his hinged wooden box.
But many don't pay, one reason or another,
and the man at the office
lets him keep just a dollar.
For his two months of Wednesdays,
early morning, late supper,
he brings his first pay to his mother in the car.
She takes the collection book, strides into the office,
says nothing going home.
No more bundles arrive.

8

The long walk from school starts to change,
his pace slowing with an ache for company.
He skips the shortcut through the railroad yard.
He lingers by the stretch of stores, stops
at the pharmacy soda fountain, meets
girls from school, walks with one or two.
One is better, he's not sure why.
There isn't much to talk about, yet they talk.
He lacks the crudity of other boys, assumes it's morality
though religion is mostly a fog to him.
This lets him stop at one girl's house,
have a treat, discuss movie stars, school.
A dull little visit except
it's *him* doing it, no one else.
At home and school he walks taller,
sensing a new balance in the world.
He's crossed some barrier not known before.

9

He waits for assistant pastor to reach his name,
hand him his report card with mundane comment.
But instead: "Why aren't you at basketball?
We could use your height."
Forty-some people watching, so he says he'll be there.
He'd rather be home, but he goes and fakes aggressiveness.
They show him some tricks for inside play,
(no need to dribble, look foolish).
The team had been losing every game but
with him they start winning, more than half.
It feels good, the aggressiveness,
but he knows it's just a role, will fade.
He'll retreat to the sidelines again,
be a mind and a soul all his own.

10

He finds high school humbling, demanding,
despite the fellowship of other adolescents.
He feels his way. He follows his schedules,
endures rowdy locker rooms, cafeteria chaos.
He studies, works hard at pleasing teachers yet
he falls short
of what the best achieve, their status as students.
A year or so in, a rare party with his peers,
most from outside his male school.
They're more relaxed than he's used to,
without compulsion, his regimented days.
To a dark-haired girl with sparkling eyes
he describes his school, activities. She's impressed.
He senses this isn't enough, though,
that the hard shell of character can exclude you.
At a science fair later he meets another girl,
blond and shy but persistent in conversation.
She draws answers from beneath his shell,
he senses a warmer response.
But they can't meet again, it turns out.
The vast metropolis lies between them,
a couple too young to manage distance.

11

His first real job, a busboy,
then dishing desserts when another is fired,
the fountain boy.
He helps when needed at the grill or wherever,
but his true role is here
with the pretty desserts,
the illusions of life rewarded,
held over from childhood.
He often samples things, gains needed weight.
He lifts waitresses' orders off a spindle,
fills them quickly,
and smiles in his role as fulfiller of dreams.

12

The long-distance run, its odd appeal,
lures him to romp through a city park
with other conflicted youths,
in and yet out of the culture's flow.
The pain, relief as it ebbs,
the meager success in meets,
but mostly brotherhood with other runners
draw him to the daily ritual.
He strains toward a goal unclear, perhaps unreal,
knowing only that it's pure,
and exulting in his sacrifice.

13

The youth, the young man stands for pictures
on finishing high school, disappointed,
a sense of hollowness at his core,
his diploma like an expired ticket,
credential for a life he doesn't want.
The "school spirit" has not been his,
his preference reading alone or
conferring with others on the fringe.
Now, the years over, he questions why:
was it him or the surroundings, the order?
Perhaps because all boys, young men—
but he shuns the simple answer, wanting more.
Plans confused, he enrolls at junior college,
male and female both, no "spirit" issue.
In fact a drift the other way: mediocrity.
A limbo, then, a resting place,
a haven from the military draft.
Yet it's another sort of order, exerting its force,
which a restless mind must soon shake off.

14

An escapee from junior college, he works in a cookie factory,
with quarter-ton barrels of shortening and margarine,
with a scraper by an oven, hundred twenty degrees,
with a question where he's going, being carried.
But among the women packing are a pair of college girls,
he noting their difference from the lifers, the drudges.
(The routine, the time-clock, clearly so suffocating.)
The girls leave for college, he talks with the boss,
quits to commute to a local university.
A strike was coming anyway, and then there's the draft,
the maelstrom pulling toward Vietnam.
He passes the picketers on frigid winter days,
people he worked with, talked and laughed with,
viewed without regret from a cozy city bus.
His courses are hard, he has trouble with the thinking,
the abstractions.
He plays pool and ping-pong when he should study Puritans.
He's placed on probation, a wake-up call,
the drum-beat of the draft growing loud, intense.
He switches to easy courses, bears down,
his grades a victory of life over death.
He still doesn't know where he's going, may never,
but he's learned there are pitfalls nonetheless.
Stay on the road, going forward, don't perish.
To live is the point of life.

15

For late afternoons in the campus library,
he has a special spot where he only half-studies,
preferring to drift mentally in the red sunlight
over the city, subdued below him.
It's poles apart from the reserve area,
where he reads rare originals of Freud,
finding them dull,
or pores over topographic maps, arcane assignments.
Different too from where he plows through novels,
leaving furrows of emotion as he spies on fake people.
No, here in the red glow his math becomes a prop,
no nourishment to his grade average.
He'll never get it anyway, after a point.
So in glory he rules the softened world outside,
its romance and wealth, its excitement,
all his as a new adult, powerful in his potential.

16

A cavernous place, the printing plant,
for ten months a balance, or ballast, in his life,
anchoring him in a sea of studies,
fear of war,
and elusive, slippery bonds with those he knows.
He meets others here where books are born,
dwellers among the presses, bindery, cutting machines,
but he starts in the quiet warehouse, packing boxes.
He meets a girl here from school, takes her out.
But hers is a different current of life,
closer to the pulsing of the factory, its dwellers.
By the time they let him go, late October,
her drift from his life is more certain,
so he relishes his release from workers' prison.

17

They'll be a forgotten factor, if factor they are at all,
the young men who meet for coffee,
cigarettes on the library stairs, talking small.
Not radicals, nor patriots, they sense a useless war but
have to keep their cars running, make some pocket money,
get by in a cold city.
Through smoke in a stairwell, one says to our man,
"There's greasers and dupers, greasers kind of bad,
well not really, all right just don't cross them.
I'm kinda in-between, but you, you're a duper:
laid-back, thinking, with those shoes—brown loafers?
Greasers' are like mine, maybe pointier, more shine."
Our man lunches with them in a room behind a bar,
sees them intense in the campus pool room,
always the pressure of the grade-point average:
stay out of war, stay in this life.

18

A rain-slicked expressway, a too slow car
drifting right at a worst possible moment
—right in front of him—
sure collision.
He swings left, no chance to look, car skidding
three-sixty and more, his thought en route:
"I'll die now," calm in its sureness.
But he's staring into headlights through his side window.
They all stopped, all lanes, and he lives.
He arrives at the house unsure what to say,
finds them by the television, stunned because
Martin Luther King was just shot, he's died.
The young man simply treasures them, the warm house,
and the secret that was his story.

19

There's an elective, classics in translation,
a prissy instructor, eight or so other students, all female,
one of them another elective for him.
A couple years younger, motherless, an immigrant,
a friendly match for the rootless, the restless.
Robert Kennedy's demise, later convention riots,
shocks no one is used to,
but for him conventional dating that's unaccustomed,
movies and concerts like it's the fifties.
He sits with her in the summer night,
or kisses her standing,
feels her old-world hug,
and imagines nothing else is happening.
Which is why it can't go on, of course.
Oh, they meet in the library in the fall,
have lunch at the pub, but
Nixon's being elected, things are happening.
It isn't a time for romantics.
For Christmastime he commits to postal work,
long surreal hours,
doesn't make it to her lake country home.
She holds him to blame but what's he to do?
His reprieve from war's insanity is wearing thin.
He can't get involved, might need to disappear.
Such is a mood engendered by war,
with the urge not to fight but survive.

20

Deferment ended, he reports for his draft physical.
A cavernous building downtown, the seedy end,
an air of male brusqueness,
bodies being shuttled, move yourself along.
Mental tests too simple to flunk, so pass or
you're passed for faking, then look out.
Stripped to underpants the rest of the way,
milling with strangers, also near-nude,
pictures of concentration camps coming to mind.
All are examined like specimens, most quickly,
but his cross-country shin gets an extra look,
the out-of-focus knee, something askew.
They urinate in cups, but it seems disorganized,
soldiers chatting, laughing as they slap labels on.
For the hearing test his earphones aren't right,
not enough beeps to mark the answer sheet, so
he takes his cues from the draftee on his left,
cheating on a test for the first time in his life.
He'll never know why, perhaps fear.
When fear is in charge, people go crazy.
At the end, dressed again, they get slips with results.
Glumness pervades, future soldiers file out.
But our man has failed badly, can't believe, slow to leave.
His service isn't required, nor even desired.
He folds away the slip as he exits,
meets the sunlight of late afternoon,
his plan to see the Quaker group dissolved,
the new life in Canada a myth of his past.

21

Though a war rages on, it's departed his consciousness,
his escape leaving a void, moon-still and pleasant.
His job on the wide office floor, claims and claimants,
a sweet banality in which he lolls,
is good for now, he thinks, but a habit builds.
The camaraderie,
the change from ties to casual,
eventually beer at breaks,
and he's maybe in a rut, not building on his luck, his potential.
She's there one day near him, foreign but frank
in her comments, her complaints.
He's cautious toward her, watching others test her temper
and her charm, ineluctable.
By default, then determination, they're lunch mates,
she on high heels on the sidewalk's ice,
he and the restaurant waiting patiently.
To match her degree, he'll return to school,
a plan he shares with her,
and decides to leave his parents, get a private place
that winter of their encounter,
their odd linking.
They have meetings, not dates, some
ordinary spark not there but
a mutual curiosity, a testing
of standards, goals, even dreams.
"You're my confidant," she says,
and glows as his inspiration.

22

On his own, working, he seeks a higher level,
enters a graduate program,
is soon wearing glasses for the first time.
With long evening classes twice a week,
other times reading, often writing,
there's not much time for the casual,
even phone calls, yet he doesn't mind.
His restlessness is absorbed, he feels direction.
Toward what, he doesn't know.
He starts to have a drink or two before class,
thinking he'll sound more profound,
tempers the effect with Chinese food.
It works and the office stiff transforms
into a reflective scholar in the night.
Nothing's without cost, of course.
Among those he doesn't call
is she who inspired this change, who
now is not as joined to him in destiny.

23

His new office, bustling and festering
amid the city's written-off wasteland,
a source of income for the working scholar,
a necessary ordeal, has few lighter moments.
But then one day comes a sunny presence,
she from California, and a coffee break together.
He drives her to lunch, they have drinks,
approach something wondrous,
more within her knowledge than his,
there in her eyes—the brightness, the thrill.
Her golden-brown hair above him in the apartment,
a curtain against the rest of the world, all knowledge
except her slim tan form swaying around him,
he reaches for her, grasping—
Grasping, yet then she dissolves in his grip.
Absent from work, not answering calls, she
drifts in a state facility, a portion of the her he's known.
There were demons in the sun she'd brought.
A surly brother and an aunt come to take her back,
the working scholar left behind,
his books again his prime companions.
A monkish chill replaces the borrowed sun.

24

He graduates at an archaic ceremony,
ponders his degree, the question why,
for what? He has no doctoral plans, no
teaching offers except New Zealand.
There's a chance to move up at the company,
supervise new hires on a special project.
He puts his advanced degree away, satisfied
he's achieved a goal, however now unclear,
however defunct.

25

He reports to the bare-bones office, a big open space,
bingo tables of hasty hires,
folding chairs for supervisors too.
Sign on coffee urn: "You no pay, you stay away."
Armed guards by entrance and manager's room,
hers the only soft chair.
The young man holds his laughter, it's a promotion after all,
a step forward in this frigid November.
The chain-smoking manager, away from comforts
of headquarters, close to chaos here,
seems to like him among her supervisors.
Perhaps from him she gains a hold, sustaining
her courage till her five-o'clock pickup.
He brings her take-out for lunch,
ignoring the wine-drinkers in a snowy car,
one or two of them his workers.
He waits to go home till manager's safely left,
a limo affording her retreat.
It's only a few months, he knows,
an initiation,
then credit for dirty work accomplished,
for keeping clean and safe her hands to raise him.

26

Convenient for a while and incredibly innocent,
his friendship with the roommates down the hall.
The younger one has her boyfriend so he's more with the other,
deeper and intriguing in her way, perhaps wounded.
She goes to church, he walks along, they visit a pub.
He makes an awkward visit to her hospital stay,
malady unknown, then plays chess with the younger one,
enjoying her homemade soup.
It's balanced, each woman a check on the other,
just friendly, not serious, not a problem for him.
But then for a college friend, another chess partner,
he accepts a blind date, completes a foursome.
She's a woman on the rebound, unattached
and yet magnetic, eyes and laugh enchanting.
Quickly, too quickly, she becomes his focus,
consuming his thoughts and energies, responsive
to his touch, endearing.
Rather suddenly, they're engaged, but
her father out of town is displeased.
She brushes aside the rejection and yet
uncertainty enters their time together,
their life down the road unclear.
She runs into an old flame, tells our man
her doubts, returns the engagement ring.
They stay close awhile but he hasn't the heart to contend,
try to salvage a reduced relationship.
His friendship with the roommates eclipsed, he can't revisit them,
again in a reduced role,
so he moves to another place, escapes.

The building smaller, newer, he meets a woman upstairs,
then her friend who needs help with a couch.
He helps carry it, they sit on it later and kiss.
She cooks a meal, dessert skipped for bedroom.
With desire strangely deep, religious, she draws him,
allows herself to be known.
He knows her in the soft light with multiple tender touches,
thinking a thank-you to his neighbor-liaison.

27

The president resigns, a useless war wears down,
prices rise, the disco beat throbs on.
Meanings wear thin, our man finds,
relationships easily passing, intimacy like
something in the wind,
nothing there to hold it, keep it solid.
Love becomes a legend.
For solidity he turns to liquor, elixir on ice,
a friend that's best when he's alone,
a best friend too often.
He has some bad mornings at work, catches himself,
plots to avoid the nightly crash.
Meaning or no, he thinks, he won't go down in flames.
His work thus saves him.

28

The working man, at the level he belongs,
where he'll be awhile, paying his expected dues,
feels drawn to diversion, to drink, yet
he pauses in memory of recent excess,
interpersonal fuss.
A second job, minor, drawing on his extra degree,
will fill the dangerous hours.
He's their teacher, then, these raw recruits
for defense of country and other purposes,
the best they can get after Vietnam.
Basic literacy their goal, reasonable yet remote,
he struggles with them thrice weekly,
enjoying the respect, appalled by the ignorance, dullness.
Is this what their officers feel?
To balance this life he responds to the hula nurse,
a chance acquaintance who lives in circles.
She'll drink a bit, she's loose, but not seeking sex.
She works extra like him but doesn't drive, needs rides.
Safe then their meetings, both tired from work:
the times in the car, short dinners, a party.
They share the smiles of escape from life's snares.
Why then, after class with the soldiers, does he
stop at the shooting place, firing round after round after round
with hardening stare and grimace at an unknown enemy?
The answer doesn't come, he keeps shooting it down.
Returning to the hula nurse, he moves to kiss her one night.
Her glow, fully warm, is eclipsed by sudden recall:
a package she meant to give him, which she fetches
and then hustles him off.

He opens the gift outside: a brand-new shower curtain.
He laughs. Liking the feel, he laughs again.
He keeps the curtain unused, in a place of honor,
toasting it when he drinks,
aware of forces beyond human change,
yet forces among which he strives.

29

The gas lines aren't as long, but prices stay up,
inflation and economy hot topics.
The man sees hiring slowed, reorganizations,
questions of authority and responsibility, bickering.
A messy sort of politics spreads, personal likes
and loyalties overwhelming objectivity.
The man doesn't care for this game but
can't combat it with credentials,
having gone for an English degree,
so promotion seems remote.
His performance, taken for granted, becomes
mostly a credential for working somewhere else.
When he dates a friend of the hula nurse,
young and princess-like, he feels
oddly unworthy.
He tries a sprightly waitress, seeking escape,
then settles on a colleague from another branch,
a divorcee. A friend for dinner. Measured love.
Easy for him now, these relationships, but
for how much longer?
The stable progress he'd assumed is gone
and with it his social predictability.
An organization less valuable to him is
less worthy of his respect and so
erodes his self-respect if he stays there.
Cut off from management, wanting to wear its mantel
in his personal life, his only decent option
is to leave.

Which he'll do in time,
in his own good time.
(Not wishing to be rushed or rousted,
or to dance to the tune of economy
and its peripatetic puppets.)

30

Timeout from the tumult,
a long distance date in San Francisco,
tall and proper in ash-blond hairdo.
Walking the hills, sampling cuisine, diversion
turning to distraction on her couch, then the floor
until she, uneasy, offers the bedroom.
She flinches there, he has to soothe her,
an unfamiliar role,
but he arches in triumph as the fog-horns blow.
She thrashes ecstatic, stops with a guilty look.
"It's all right," he tells her.
Liberated, she stands in the morn emboldened,
talks casually, proud of her adjustment.
Another night with her, then he takes one off,
watching football when she calls and gets miffed,
the relationship ending over breakfast—
eggs for him, tears for her.

31

A sort of wasteland fills his dreams,
sandy and endless,
the continuing end of the preceding day,
with gusts that settle in the dawn.
Humid summer nights with parties full of strangers,
even new friends remaining strangers.
Even with autumn chill, then snow,
the gap remains,
nothing clicking to create a team, a couple.
His friendships falter, he feels an ache,
youth passing.
The old recklessness no longer works, he sees,
something else is needed.
His manner subsides, he sees people from afar,
their home base, their stability.
From the sandy waste of his dreams he sees their cities,
the arabesque pattern of their activities.

32

His neighbor across the landing, single middle-aged male,
hurries downstairs to work on a frigid morning.
Our man hears him, feels cozier in his bed,
using another of his backlogged off-days,
on the road to quitting and roads beyond that.
Coffee made, sunlight glowing through the frost,
he sits at table with a brochure before him.
The business school is new, pending accreditation,
so he could slide in now and jump-start his career.
He sits back, takes a sip, gazes into
winter light, its insouciance.
Dust particles float, can await forever his answer.
Yes but, he thinks, and sees himself
stepping into limbo, a vacuum,
taking a leap of faith, a gamble.
Perhaps just a different company, more solid,
with work more important, demanding so
he can shine, move up like he knows he should.
Later he leaves to drive his car,
warm and charge the battery.
He'll warm it again that night,
not wanting to gamble with the cold.

33

The man travels to Europe, visits the postcard sites:
museums, castles, cathedrals, symphony halls.
He sees where battles were fought, where vineyards lie,
generations of blood and wine in soil beneath his feet.
Such history, such pathos and beauty, yet
somehow there's a shallowness to it.
For him anyway, as he looks at people, their faces.
People here are used to these things, are focused more
on their work, families, the ordinary day-to-day.
It's just the same old gallery of faces,
only so many human traits to go around.
Behind the postcards then, no matter what displayed,
are people needing homes, support of some kind,
desiring to be safe, secure in basic ways.
The man, out strolling, stops to view a river,
the European life around it.
Interesting, he thinks, but he won't miss it,
because its heart has its twin back home.

34

A certain season of life, the settling down,
provokes within the man a different restlessness,
a need for anchor, company at home,
some meaning in the night beyond himself.
He might have passed through this stage,
already confirmed bachelor to most,
but he senses that he might lose part of life,
its awareness, perhaps its essence,
and so he takes a wife.
Suddenly and secretly, it happens.
It brings comfort in normalcy, matching his peers,
and benefits of the practical sort,
but he learns there's more down the road, unseen.
For a man of order and introspection, newly calm
after the fire of youth,
the habits and hidden thoughts of another,
her accumulating needs,
can turn the settled season to a blanket of fallen leaves.

35

A sudden slowing of life can happen,
where the priority is to reflect and plan,
confined by commitment to another,
the obligations of the settling man.
As discussion wears thin, he's still with her
in all the quiet, peaceful places
where by his nature he'd be alone, or in
casual company, a light-hearted mood.
But this is solemn, even when they smile.
There's no escape. This is marriage.
They return from a meal and a walk in the park
to permanence,
a new reality that has him guessing.

36

Fatherhood, he can't quite grasp it,
an eternal identity based on an instant,
unplanned or uncertain, indiscretion or hope.
It ties him to a future, he knows,
more tightly even than marriage,
behind the gush of joy many shadows,
more obstacles and closing doors.
No choice for a man of character but accept,
and so he does, working long
and strongly in the sunset of his youth.

37

He sometimes misses the beers at lunch,
fictional field calls, careless conflicts
and other follies of his previous work.
But this is an investment, he tells himself,
of maturing ability in his family's future,
which he could not escape if he wanted to, so
must therefore strive to build, enhance, ensure.
The company is sound. He works in good faith.
Why should he then not succeed?
Nevertheless, on the way to his homeward train,
he buys a cocktail to go, in styrofoam cup,
to be sipped as city neighborhoods whiz by,
easing the restless sense of something left behind.

38

Suede-jacketed, he stands on winding private road,
old-fashioned in hand,
directing distant relatives where to park.
Standing in the cold,
the big house behind him with snowy lawn,
the trees still bare,
he smiles in his festive task.
A rare item, this party for his parents,
their special anniversary, a surprise.
As they drive up, the big house quiets,
he directs them to a space before the door,
watching, with a quiet sip of liquor,
the world and generations move along.

39

A trip to a foreign land, a dictatorship,
to clean up another's mess, a man now fired.
"Just do the research," the manager says.
"We'll analyze when you get back."
And so he goes.
He meets the welcoming smiles, the fancy meals,
rides briskly past mounds of garbage, children searching in it.
He tries to study business, the books
and explanations,
but is nagged by a sense that he's in a game,
on the defensive,
principles being compromised amid the unknown.
They send a girl to his room, young,
maybe underage back home.
She's pretty in the weak light, the humid quiet,
and he's tempted but
his memories of an assignment, stern manager, fired forebear,
the need to progress for distant family,
are a gulf between him and the girl,
a protection for now, this night.
They talk awhile and then she leaves, at first
refusing money for her family, then accepting.
Back home he presents his findings, omitting the girl.
The manager is pleased: "You'll move up the ladder,"
he says, but also that
he himself is moving, a transfer to the West Coast.
So fades the luster of one's achievement,
lost to the views of later people.

40

Poised on the step to management,
he's asked to mentor one last time:
an attractive woman, bright, cultured,
commuting from an upscale suburb.
She catches on quickly, is fun to talk with,
could be handled by someone junior,
why him?
Maybe as a reward, preparation
for coming privileges, management life.
His reviews of her work grow cursory, a normal thing,
her conclusions and advice most important.
They have drinks a few times at the station but
that's as far as it goes,
the long leash of his family role
restraining him from dalliance.

41

Entering the room, sees his boss with an auditor,
sees trouble but is puzzled, sits softly.
Yes, he tells them, he reviews the new one's work.
"But A, B, and C, all parts of her reports?"
She got the hang of A, then B, so he's down to checking C.
"The C here would be fine except the A is not,
is bogus,
so the B then the C are falsehoods."
He pictures the long-haired young specialist, so bright.
He had no idea, have they talked with her?
"She's already fired," says the boss,
the woman from auditing silent.
A sense of something off, unreal in the room, so he asks
within the blip whether he's fired, too.
"Not fired, but this happened on your watch.
You have to understand this, as we do."
Awareness, knowledge of blame, internalizing,
the way to accepting consequences, taking a hit,
taking it for the firm.
But nowhere to go here now, and no longer
a man alone, no longer young.
With a vacuum now in his life, already drifting,
he lacks a move to make and yet
he'll make one.
He has that on them:
a penchant, deep within, for the radical.

42

The man rents a cabin with state park nearby,
takes the family, stands in an ancient lake,
the work of glaciers and such.
Surrounded by pines and other trees,
a cliff on one side, it seems
the center of something, a peace
he's somehow missed in life.
Thinking back, there was summer camp as a boy,
others in charge as he is now.
But that's the thing.
He's in charge, isn't he, of decisions
that decide his fate, and now his family's?
So why has he been off-center,
missed the mark,
this tranquility that should be every day?
They drive that evening through insect song
to a cool restaurant, ice tinkling in drinks.
He smiles flatly, gaze sweeping other patrons,
wondering how many have hit the mark.

43

He'd seen her unexpectedly before,
chance encounter on downtown street,
her beauty mature in smart business suit,
not girlish like at the old apartments.
Twelve years now since those days.
At his desk on a frigid business day, she calls,
invitation to lunch, tone of purpose to her voice,
not flighty, nor tentative from her husband's shadow.
They're divorced, he learns, and divorced she appears
with a certain lack of glow,
melancholy through her brave front.
They meet again, she shows him poetry, quite personal,
they kiss, seek another room in her sparsely furnished house.
On another meeting their dinner runs late,
the restaurant's location a challenge to her memory.
He arrives home to a child's question: "Where were you?"
He needn't answer but wonders, where have I been?
What is the benefit? The risk?
Do I want to follow her down that path,
the gloom that blocks the light,
the dark joys that melt before a child's question?
A few more calls, an unsigned card, and
the healing sands drift over their affair.

44

The house, not big, stands among pines and snow,
a symbol no less than a place to live.
But early in his fifth decade,
enabled to buy through a change of jobs,
the man isn't sure: symbol of what?
Freedom of a sort, security, though
mortgage and upkeep take a toll.
Mostly it shows time passing, a stage of life
delayed for him but inevitable, at least
since the choice of marriage.
They'll plant a garden here, have a dog,
answer to no landlord and yet,
for a man his age,
it's still a matter of shelter, not a dream.
A symbol then of reality, where he's arrived in life,
perhaps a monument to it.

45

A bubbling of emotion lingers but subsides
in the rows of empty desks before him,
seated at his own battered desk, windows open
to a sunny sports field, insects in the air.
What's he have, five minutes or less
to get his coaching self out there?
The private school blinked at his credentials, meager,
but gives him duties going well beyond the bell.
They'll be trickling out, mostly boys,
a couple of hardy girls,
aching to feast on the fall afternoon.
He, man with whistle, keeping order, instructs
them in the game but really just
makes it sweeter for them to cut loose.
If only he'd understood that at his real jobs:
that he wasn't going to change anything,
that there was a game to play.
But it couldn't happen because
he needed to change something in himself
and couldn't,
as surely as he rises now above battered desk,
whistle and coaching hat in hand.

46

A good stretch of time now, making him forget
things will always change, people grow much different.
With nothing up the ladder he moves laterally,
changing jobs to gain flexibility,
time to plant roses, coach his son's teams.
The marriage gains a tenuous normalcy,
best when viewed through garden branches
or in restaurants, their neutrality.
He can live for today, maybe has to, but knows
he's only on a parallel track with those
who are also going far, but are higher.
The passing years, his tree of choices, his nature,
shortages of strengths of different sorts,
have left him a decent citizen, but scrambling.

47

The man shows houses, selling one now and then,
soon enough to go full-time.
Another career, another set of tasks,
dealing more with greed than reason,
using his flexibility.
Old frame types his specialty,
he puffs their charm, affordability,
pooh-poohing flaws and flimsiness, symptoms
of obsolescence,
any value-changing evidence
of a property's senescence.
He likes the hours, flexible, though calls
come at any time,
with pressure at the closings, people edgy.
There's time to reflect, often more than he likes,
on the life that brought him to this, this hustling.
He never *wanted* to sell, convince people,
clip the picture's tattered corners.
He wanted to be of service, liked, things
falling in place, with well-earned rewards.
It's how his colleagues see *this* job,
he knows, and he's again the outsider.
On a worn-out carpet of lawn, he awaits his buyer,
viewing the empty house, passage for humble families.
A stirring of wind, he looks skyward,
sensing the chamber of his own passage:
the working world in which he's a lighter cog.

48

His mother dies suddenly, not quite in her sleep,
waking with the dawn to watch it slip away.
Strange reversal, yet not a night-ending dream
she knows, calling out a name, murmuring prayers.
No warning, she's been healthy, leaving in fact
as one would leave a dream,
fading out and into a new, hidden reality.
The man and his relations wonder at this and yet
soon become aware of their own new reality.
She was after all at the center of things,
the strongest bond among them,
their ties now becoming tentative, infrequent.
The funeral is on a cool summer day,
cool though the sun is bright, glaring.
The plot next to hers awaits her aging spouse.

49

Crouching in the garden behind the house,
the odd corner between garage and fence,
he smiles at evening sunshine off the tomatoes,
the sublime peace he feels, though only for now.
Why can't it continue? Modest though it is,
their life's been fairly stable, normal for a while.
But something within her follows opportunity,
a pull too strong for him or their home to match.
And so one day he stands with son and dog,
watching her back her car, waving,
and off she goes to her distant employment,
while back they stay at the site of separation.
"We'll see her some weekends," he says as they stand.
The garden has a different feel now,
the sunshine futile in the fall,
having the best replaced by
making the best you can
of separation.

50

A man of promise once, he drifts from job to job,
one set of faces to the next,
with which he must deal.
He's learned to keep moving to avoid the rut,
the pit of apathy and desperation
that breeds friction, workplace defeat.
Well through his fifth decade, he can't afford showdowns,
two or three years and he's gone.
It's his limit on handling a set of faces,
the echoes in them of his failure.
Now he fails at even this modest goal,
problems mount just a few months in.
They don't understand him, he thinks, no one does.
They don't know his home life, disappointments,
his early belief—unquestioned—in his greatness
(appreciation just a matter of time).
Well, time has passed, and passed and passed
and his only hope lies outside him.
The job is covered by a union of sorts,
weak but an obstacle to firing,
giving time to find a nest elsewhere,
cushioning for his fall.
Survival, he thinks, still his talent after all,
as close as he'll come to greatness.

51

The second home, though bigger, is
not a statement like the first,
that monument to choices, fetishes and follies.
The lot is bigger too, unfenced, suggesting
sharing of interests with stable neighbors.
Again a passage of time, a point in life,
but the rearward view is long, gets dim.
The man maintains the house, relates to those around,
even has a party, then has more,
yet always that unease that much is wrong.
He's pushing a limit, he sees, in playing
these social roles, his phantom self
still lurking in that shade of his mental grove.
(Always an urge to play the pipes, erupt in outrageous song,
dance on a summer night across fragrant unfenced lawns!)

52

In lapses in the day's activity, or late at night,
our man reflects on what he's missed in life.
The material, professional, and social come to mind,
but then a higher plane, the arts, looms large.
Responding, he views paintings, reads poetry,
gives classical music an unbiased ear.
He finds he appreciates talent, the work,
senses the realities of visions,
but is somehow shut out from knowing,
from entering artists' dimension.
It bothers him to think he's stunted,
rooted in banality that engulfs his days,
but then sees it as a matter of degree.
At least he knows the value, he tried
more than most around him ever do.
This tempers his reflections on what he's missed,
easing his return from the higher plane
which, anyway,
has so little influence in this, our world.

53

Working now in a shelter, midnight shift,
admitting people from the fringes of life,
the man measures his own distance from chaos.
The rages of the night, spawning refugees, are
rough shores he might be drifting toward.
It seemed a good move, his coming here, an escape
from the harsh demands of postal work, physical
and spiritual assaults on his age and temperament.
Yet now, his shift wearing on,
he sees a coldness in the dawn,
no coming glory just an empty chill.
There's little more for him in work,
this working world,
so only in the margins can he live
with one eye on the edge.

54

The man gets a transfer to day work,
leaving the muddled night world behind.
A relief at first, some normalcy at home,
but he soon senses deeper problems,
a ballooning void where purpose once lived,
thinning relevance in the papers he moves,
dull succinctness in his computer entries.
There's an age thing in the office, unspoken
yet clear in the light of day, undeniable.
He struggles a few months but sees trouble ahead:
budget cuts, a fall. He gives notice instead.
And why not? His son's off to college,
he's alone in the house with a declining dog.
He can move to end marital separation.
So with hope more than planning he cuts his ties,
drives off one day when the house sale clears
through flurries of snow to the Interstate.

55

In a different state, a different population,
his different stage of life is reinforced,
overlays his fading momentum,
the remnants of ambition to escape,
start over.
A call comes in, he doesn't pick up, listens
to the machine: an offer to interview.
He sometimes calls back, keeps appointments,
even agrees to work, almost starts.
Always the same thing nagging, a sense that
this isn't real, he doesn't belong here.
His routine is from the place he left,
doesn't mesh with these people,
and it's all getting old: his routine, his style.
Without all systems go, dragging doubts,
he's enticed by the thought of quitting—
informal, abnormal retirement.
And why not?
He has savings, shares her house,
seeks no identity through work roles, goals,
all the stifling folderol.
He eases on applications, his ersatz search,
finds turn-downs reassuring, liberating.
Not employed or supervised, without imposed goals,
he's freed as an individual, he thinks,
something that should've happened long ago.
It should've been his life, rather than the servitude
that kept him running
in the labyrinth of sterile industry.

He spends more time in the yard, sleeps long hours,
catches ball games on TV, buys a bike.
A solitary cyclist, he drifts through local parks,
wide straw hat tipped low, peering out,
staying on the move to avoid a weirdo look.

56

The man's father passes away, up in years as he'd say.
The old siblings and their peers see his time had come,
so theirs has also, almost
(the never-ceasing shock of mortality).
For the next generation, our man and his siblings,
the father is gone, yes, but he always partly was.
For our man, especially, the link was weak,
son and father not sensed in each other.
The last few years, dementia, the father's puzzled look,
not knowing the son or even that he'd had any.
With his death another stage, then, in non-recognition:
not even that expression for the son to search
for something in the past that made sense,
made a bond.
A raw winter's day for the funeral, some snowflakes,
mourners not mourning but showing respect.

57

The man is hired by a community college,
emergency recruit from back applications.
He'll teach a class in tech writing, qualified
by his degree from long before:
a young man poring over Keats and Dickens,
unraveling Joyce in the still hours of night.
So it's business letters now, reports, proposals,
emails and instructions for products. Well.
He taught the navy recruits, and then in middle school,
so maybe this is no worse fit.
But he finds he mostly repeats the text,
some students nodding off,
his voice often strained.
From a roster of twenty he ends up grading five,
two with missing work he overlooks.
The college makes no mention of further classes,
does not call again for his services.
The man feels the end of his teaching career
and, peering through blinds at a new day,
of his time in the work world as well.

58

He should be involved with something—
work, volunteering, a hobby.
But instead he awaits full retirement,
functionless,
squinting out at nature, feeling
a new knowledge of it, smiling
despite the hot sun.
Geese waddle near the creek, he walks his bike
to the shade of a tree, sits.
A lull in his life's activity but
there must be a purpose, mustn't there?
Maybe to be ready for something,
that elusive greatness of his youthful hopes.
But he laughs, surprising himself.
There needn't be greatness, or any purpose at all,
to have this lull. Nor potentiality.
It's for him what it is for those geese, this tree:
an absence of something happening so
just a now, an existence.
He sits a long while, letting the sun shift.
This might as well be his living room, he thinks,
these creatures his family and friends.

59

Dissolution, the word jumping out from the pages,
nowhere calling it divorce,
just dissolution, like solid settling in liquid,
no longer in solution.
No longer *a* solution, that could be.
Finding a solution was why he sought marriage,
it being no accident, nor something inevitable.
The central chunk of his life, decades
defined by what's now dissolved—
so now what meaning for those years?
Dissolution, he sees, was the part inevitable,
as with other dying illusions
that nourish a legion of lawyers.
Dissolution, disillusion, sibling sounds.
What seemed to solve his life, its needs,
was flawed,
played out into these papers in his hands.
No more need for reasons along the way
than for seeking special grains among the sands.

60

On his own again, single man in apartment.
Grocery shopping for one, mailbox in the wall
of a lobby with vending machines, newspaper piles.
A motel feel to life. Just passing through.
But to where?
The laundry room, washers and dryers rumbling.
An institutional feel to life.
He looks back in memory to his youth,
his handling this so easily,
exulting in it.
Has he declined somehow in character, feeling
burdened by a life that once gave hope?
He doesn't know. He has his life experience
so he should be better. But he doesn't know.
Instead he buys quality wines,
slices cheese on a plate with crackers and
listens to classical music in the after-sunset glow.

61

Getting up in the dark, bizarre break in routine,
rediscovering the crisp chill of dawn,
he finds the town courthouse for his long-avoided role.
He's searched, guided around, and he waits,
mulling the reasons he should not judge.
Get out of it, always his goal in the end.
But picky though they are they never reach his name,
the jury is filled and he's dismissed
unheard from,
fifteen dollars richer
and free to face his vacant hours alone.

62

Thirty years since he hit the West Coast,
but he's there now to visit his brilliant son,
earning twice what the man, the father, ever made.
The hills of a pleasant city test his walking,
the hotel room tests his endurance of memories.
An old building in a popular area, with
an aging man at a window looking down
at people mostly younger, many much younger,
mostly much younger with life's full schedule,
full repertoire, full dreams.
When he leaves it will be another memory
to add to the load he struggles to justify
yet treasures as conscious life, his self.

63

Back in the town where things didn't work,
he sees that it's time to move on.
Visits to the son and others aren't enough,
he must leave the failed connections here,
the sense of stagnancy that isolation breeds.
Though retired, he might see many seasons yet
in his journey with the earth through time, the universe.
He doesn't know what the seasons will bring but
for him that's value: unfolding awareness.
He should treasure every one of them
until time runs out.
Never good at good-byes, this man, whether
in person, telephone, in writing, computer—
something always seems unspoken, unfinished
that should have been done.
So without much planning he moves far away,
abruptly to some, arbitrarily,
yet answering again the call to be born.

THE CELESTIAL OPERA

1

I had to attend the wake for Edward, an old school chum, even though I hadn't seen him for many years. I'd often thought of him with his engaging good humor, mixed with surface irritation, and regretted he was among the many with whom I'd lost touch. The funeral parlor was quite full when I arrived but this didn't surprise me. Edward had maintained many contacts since he tended to work in two or three professions at once. He was an editor of trade publications who became an insurance agent on the side and then got into real estate. The latter field eventually provided his primary income, but he was also a musician and played regularly with a small band at various functions.

Having paid my respects, I stood awhile in the crowd of people unknown to me, considering when I should leave. It was then that I spotted a familiar face and form moving uncertainly across the room. Though another I hadn't seen in years, I realized at once that it was Florian, with whom Edward and I had attended commuter college. It was during a hiatus in Florian's career as a monk. He'd left his calling for a while to experience the wider world, finding himself a niche as manager of an urban apartment building. The tenants were a diverse lot with many foibles and follies. Florian had entertained me with their stories, which I later discreetly utilized in my writing.

We greeted each other warmly, both of us surprised and pleased.

"Quite a distance for you," I said. "Did you drive?"

"No, I came by train. Going back tomorrow after the funeral. Just a two-day leave."

"Ah, so they've learned not to trust you."

"It's by mutual agreement, believe me. No more odysseys of discovery. I'm too old and the world's too out of control. Has been for some time."

I glanced around the funeral parlor.

"Speaking of which, our occasion here is becoming a cross between *Finnegan's Wake* and *The Last Hurrah*."

"Yes, it is rather raucous."

"There's a pub of some sort across the street. Better stuff, no doubt, than what our fellow mourners have in their pockets."

"No doubt, yes. Let's be off."

We picked our way through the crowd and out the congested entrance. The old snow and slush were already freezing along the city street, but the neon sign on the pub blinked invitingly: "Lenehan's." We had just enough taste of the cold to appreciate again the warmth of indoors, along with the mouth-watering aromas of beverages we both loved.

"J.J. or Bushmills?" asked the bartender.

"No Paddy's?" Florian kidded.

Our man ignored him and reached for the J.J. We each had just one and then went to a table with our beers. The place was more than half full, with substantial spillover from the funeral parlor. Edward's mourners were the loudest present.

"You'd hardly know it's the twenty-first century," I observed.

"Yes, it's turned into quite a party."

"Edward would've wanted it so, don't you think?"

"I suppose he would," my companion said pensively.

I knew the look he'd taken on, that he was recollecting. And not about Edward, I guessed. Florian was rich in experience despite his reclusiveness. I awaited his statement.

"This reminds me of the bar near the building I managed," he said. "I was there a few times with McGonigle, the janitor. There was one time something like tonight. Not after a death, exactly—a near death, yes, but that worked out—but the mood in the bar was like tonight, kind of melancholy sweet."

"So, not quite everything worked out?"

He hunched forward, squinted into middle distance.

"The thing is, there are effects left by near death, or a threat of death—the amplified fear—that can mar or scar people's lives. Warp the course of events that follow. I was thinking of Chub and Pete. Did I tell you about them?"

"No. I'm sure I would've remembered the names."

"Let me tell you now."

And he proceeded to do so, his account discreetly utilized later in my writing.

2

Chub lived on the second floor, just below Florian and just above the janitor, McGonigle. Chub lifted weights and was careless in the lowering, dropping the barbell like a wrecking ball. The country music he played did little to cover the crash. When exercising, or anytime during summer, he'd wear only jockey shorts and leave his doors wide open. For air, he told Florian—to increase the aerobic effect. He also aired his garbage, leaving it on the porch—unwrapped—for the janitor to pick up.

"Another boob," was McGonigle's appraisal. "A real bust-out. Why don't you give him the notice, Florry?"

As building manager, Florian served the requests to vacate.

"Can't do it, Jack. You know Mr. Needlenose. As long as the rent comes in, a tenant is all right."

"Yeah, all right for him it is. Out there in the 'burbs on a street named after him. He don't get the wrath of God from a boob upstairs dropping weights."

Fortunately, Chub worked nights. The noise and displays would cease and tranquility could descend. But his presence during the day was a lure to another tenant, a very small one. Pete was a boy of five or six who lived in a one-bedroom off the front of the courtyard. His mom, as Pete called her, was much lighter than the boy, and seemed moody to Florian. He sensed a long, sad story that had brought her to Basil Street. But Florian had his own problems, including keeping a job here, so he avoided Pete and his mom except for business. This left Chub as fair game for the curious little boy.

"What you doing there?" he called in to Chub.

"Exercising."

"What that music? Sound like bottle-nose."

"Bottle-nose? Who's that?"

"Man down on curb. Mom call him bottle-nose. Sing 'cause he drunk."

Chub turned the stereo off.

129

"You live around here?"

"Up front. We on second floor, too. But we got more space, not so full of junk. Why you just wear underpants, man?"

"I like to. It feels good. Where's your mother at?"

"She home typing. She gonna be a doctor."

"What about you? What're you gonna be?"

Pete named a professional ballplayer.

"Then I buy the ice cream store," he added.

"You want ice cream? I've got some here—toffee bars. Or do you have to ask your mother?"

"Gimme," said Pete. "I ask her later."

The boy came by every day after that, Florian hearing the music go off and a lively banter ensue. He saw them one night at a street carnival, Pete talking excitedly to Chub while his mother walked behind. Her name was Lenore, and Florian figured she welcomed any help with Pete, from a boob or otherwise. He doubted it would go any further than that until he saw her in the laundry room one day, crying as she sorted some clothes.

"Something the matter?" he asked.

"Oh, I didn't see you. No, nothing's wrong. I was just remembering my mother. The laundry reminded me again, as it reminded her of my father. They're both gone now, but she kept washing his clothes after he died. Sometimes she'd even put them on to make a reason. She was devastated, see. My brother was MIA in Vietnam. Her whole world was falling apart."

"Very sad. Hard for you too, of course."

"I was just another problem for her. But never mind. I shouldn't be telling you all this. Sorry I'm being so silly."

"No, that's all right. If you're upset, it's good to have someone—well, to talk to."

He watched her dab her eyes, saw a glow of gratitude, knew he wanted out.

"Like your son talks to Chub," he added. "They're becoming real buddies, I guess."

"How is he, do you think? All right?"

She hadn't seemed to care before, Florian thought. But all right at what exactly? He decided not to pursue it, not to get involved.

"I don't think he'd do Pete any harm," he said.

"No, neither do I. He took us to the funfair and they got on famously."

"Famously?"

She giggled as if she'd been caught at something, turned back to the laundry with a lingering smile. She wanted to be a doctor, Pete had said, raise her station in life. She'd raise it through language, typing papers, taking exams. Hard to see where Chub fit in, though.

"You gonna be my daddy?" Pete asked.

"You already got a daddy," said Chub.

"Mom don't know where he at."

"Nothing I can do about that, Pete."

"Yeah, there is. You can marry her, man."

"Hey, now. You're too young to talk like that."

"I ain't too young. I talked since I was two. One. Half o' one."

"I believe you," said Chub.

There were times, even when he wasn't working, that Chub was out. Pete had trouble accepting this. He'd bang on Chub's door for five to ten minutes, demanding ice cream or challenging Chub to a fight.

"I can beat you, man! Lifting weights just make you *pretty*! Tough is different!"

Most of Chub's outings were for country music, but he'd also shoot pool at Kelly's, a neighborhood pub. He was there one weekend when McGonigle had dragged Florian in to be his drinking partner.

"The boob's in the back room," said McGonigle.

"Chub?"

"Anyone else would be *a* boob. He's *the* boob."

Florian nodded.

"Want to invite him over?"

McGonigle laughed.

"We don't see enough of 'em, eh? Him and his welfare brat?"

Florian said nothing, hiding in beer foam his lack of a smile. He didn't like pejoratives, in jokes or otherwise.

"I have to talk to him now," he said.

"What, about the noise you mean? Nah, stow some pints, Florry! Check out the boob on Needlenose's time."

"No, there's something else, something bothering me. I won't be long."

He moved away, taking his stein with him. He passed through swinging doors to the green-topped pool tables. Chub glanced up but kept playing.

"Chub," Florian said, "that boy who's been coming around. Have you talked much with his mother?"

"Lenore? Nothing special there, Florian. She's got a lot of miles on her. A *lot* of miles."

"The boy gets upset when he finds you're out. Bangs on the door and yells. Seems like he's real attached to you."

"Yeah, I guess so."

"It might be tough breaking off, Chub. Seems you should have an understanding with Lenore. She might have expectations of her own. See, I saw her once in the laundry room and we talked. She's had a rough life, Chub."

He glanced up. The pool cue was suspended in space.

"You think she's using Pete to get to me?"

"Not intentionally, no. But things happen, you know, and people under pressure tend to grab at straws."

"Thanks a lot, man."

"I meant the chance for a serious relationship—the remote chance."

"Yeah, that's me all right—the straw man. But what do you think about her, Florian? Is she all right?"

"All right? That's not for me to say, Chub. She's not bad looking. Kind of pretty when you look close."

"Yeah. Funny, isn't it? Most women it's just the opposite. Must be the eyes, the nice skin. Shadows just right."

He went back to his pool-playing, his stroke a little crisper, more precise. Florian left him and went back to McGonigle at the bar.

"You tell the boob what to do?" the janitor asked.

"Yes," said Florian, "I think I did."

Pete didn't come by much after that, but he didn't need to. Chub was taking a closer look at Lenore so he spent a lot of time at their apartment. He didn't lift the weights as much and seemed to control them better. He even played his music lower, as if not wanting to miss something—a voice, a soft knock. He wore running shorts now, sometimes even a tee-shirt. Lenore would tend to accompany Pete when he came to Chub's apartment.

"I have some typing for tomorrow," she'd say.

"Sure. I'll take him to the park."

"Would you like the cube steak tonight?"

"Fine, but easy on the pepper this time."

McGonigle thought this was great, judging from the noise reduction, but Florian was worried. Chub was a man of creature comforts, going with what provided them. This meant Lenore for now, but what about later—when Chub started missing the pool room, got tired of baby sitting?

For Lenore, he wasn't just a fling. She needed permanence. She'd drifted a long time and was coming in to shore. Would Chub cut the rope and send her off again? Would there be scenes, with Pete caught in the middle and everyone depressed? It might get ugly, Florian thought. Even tragic.

3

One day, as Florian had feared, the police cars came. The focus was Lenore's apartment—no surprise. As building manager, he had to approach the scene, facilitate chaos so it could run its course quickly. But as Florian reached the apartment, he saw that he'd somehow been wrong. Chub and Lenore were worried—not angry—and Pete was not in the middle of things. He wasn't even there.

"I fell asleep," Chub was saying. "The big tree by the tennis courts. I wake up and he's nowhere around."

He'd returned from the park thinking he'd find Pete at home. But Lenore was alone—then frantic.

"Did you see him by Chub's?" she asked Florian.

"No, I'm afraid not."

The scene was just stabilizing when more police rushed in. Pete had been found, they said, but he was injured. He'd been thrown from a dump truck, apparently, and was found unconscious. An ambulance was taking him to the hospital.

"Oh, my God!" said Lenore. "It's happening again! It's all starting up again!"

"How could I—be—" Chub blurted.

"It's all falling apart! He's gone! I know he's gone!"

Lenore sank down in a chair while Chub looked around like a madman. Fearful, thought Florian, maybe waiting to be arrested. But the police were busy getting Lenore to the hospital. Chub wanted to go, too, but the police would only take Lenore.

"We can use McGonigle's pickup," Florian offered.

"You've got the keys?"

"I'll get them."

They were close, Florian thought, and Chub would be a comfort to Pete if he were conscious. But McGonigle wasn't sensitive to this, sourly standing in his doorway as he mulled the request for keys. He finally gave in to please Florian, but insisted he would drive.

"The boob rides in back," he said.

This might have bothered Chub, but he didn't show it. He climbed in the tailgate and sat behind them with knees drawn up. Florian could see him through the window but tried not to look. Chub was pathetic now, he thought, and should suffer in private. Even McGonigle stopped talking about him, complaining instead about potholes and the current mayor.

They got to the hospital and found Lenore. She was arguing with a doctor while a nurse and the police looked on.

"But can't you use his *own* blood?" she asked. "Isn't it regenerating all the time?"

The doctor assured her a transfusion was necessary.

"But I just can't trust those blood bottles. I know the people who gave it. They're dope addicts, bums, with AIDS and everything else!"

"The blood is all tested, ma'am. And you're lucky we have your son's type. It's not real common and supplies are low just now."

"I can't do it," said Lenore. "I won't give consent. Things are falling apart and I'm going to lose him, but I won't just sign his life away. Why don't you find a donor? Someone I can see and know they're all right. Then maybe I can sign!"

The doctor explained that there wasn't time. They had to operate *now*, he said.

"I can't," said Lenore. "No, I won't. It's wrong to infect such a nice little boy—my son—with those disgusting viruses. I'm losing him, but at least he'll be healthy in heaven!"

She started sobbing, wailing. The doctor looked angry.

"What blood type is he?" asked Florian.

"O negative."

Nothing I can do, then, Florian thought. But as he mentally washed his hands, his eyes were drawn to Chub, who'd started at hearing the blood type.

"*I'm* an O negative," he said.

Everyone looked at him, Lenore through watery eyes.

"Are you willing to serve as a donor?" the doctor asked.

"Yes. Whatever it takes to save him."

Lenore stared at him, pathetically wan.

"You're not just saying that—are you, Chub? About the blood type, I mean. It's got to be the same, you know."

"Want to see my I.D.? The blood type's *on* it."

He took a card out of his wallet and Lenore scrutinized it. McGonigle shuffled his feet and leaned close to Florian.

"They should test the boob anyway. He's a hoof-and-mouth case if I ever seen one."

But Lenore gave her approval and Chub was led away. They'd begin the procedure at once, the doctor said. The group in the hall was relieved of conflict and could only wait. They drifted off to a sitting room, the police and McGonigle soon leaving. Florian was left with Lenore—her sole comfort in spite of his need for distance.

"I heard you were a monk once," she said.

She's seeking her own distance, he thought, from worries about Pete. Maybe Chub, too.

"Yes," he said. "I'm still adjusting to civilian life."

She managed a smile. Her eyes were clear and blue when they weren't swollen. Her walnut hair, wavy but cut short, seemed to complement her chunky figure. The shadows were right, as Chub had said, making her pretty when you looked close.

"Did they lock you in there?" she asked.

"Not with a key, or with bars on the windows. We were locked in by fear."

"You were punished for things?"

"Not fear of punishment. Fear of loss. The company of brother monks. The peaceful, easy life."

"It was easy?"

"When you got used to it. Anyhow, that's gone now. I didn't fit in. Now I have freedom to deal with."

Lenore looked down, perhaps sensing his discomfort. He thought the discussion was closed. But avoidance of the present made her thoughtful again.

"I never thought of freedom as a problem," she said. "I thought it was great. I exulted in it. I defied the world by any means I could. Pete's father was one."

She looked up at him, but then back down when she saw no reaction.

"It was murder for my parents. Damnation. But I love Pete. He's all I have now, all that gives meaning to—"

But her tone was hollow, as if she were trying to convince herself. Florian doubted that she saw much meaning in things.

"I'm sure Pete will be all right," he said.

And they continued their vigil, helpless amid the clinical reality. Pete was kept at the hospital, of course, but Chub was released. They had to get a cab since McGonigle had left, Lenore sitting between them en route to the building.

"Thanks," she said to Chub. "We'll always appreciate it."

But that was as far as it went. Chub may have felt faint, and Lenore drained, but that was all they said on the way to Basil Street. Florian saw them to their apartments, saying he'd check in later, then retired to his humble cell. It seemed a week since he'd left it.

Pete came home about two weeks later. He had a cast on one arm and wore a brace, but was otherwise mobile. He wasn't as talkative and mostly stayed in his apartment. Chub went to see him a couple of times but then left off, content to lift weights again. He refrained from dropping them, though, and kept his apartment doors closed. The country music was no longer heard.

While Lenore let Florian know how Pete was healing, she seemed to have no contact with Chub. When the brace and cast were removed and Pete wanted Chub to see him, Lenore asked Florian to be there.

"I'd feel better," she said. "After the other time, I mean."

"Can't you just go yourself?"

"No, that wouldn't be right. Not after the hospital—what I put him through and all."

"I'm sure Chub understands."

"No, it wouldn't be right."

So Florian perched on the landing outside his door, hanging over the scene as Pete returned to his old haunt.

"I'm all better, man," he said to Chub.

"Hey, all right! Way to go!"

"It's 'cause of you. You saved me."

"No way, Pete. The doctors saved you."

"You gave your blood. It's in me now. I'd be dead without it."

"Forget it, Pete."

"No. I gonna save you, too. Pay you back, man. I'll pull you out of the lake."

"I'm a good swimmer, Pete."

"Then I'll shoot a bear trying to eat you."

"All right. I'll let you know when I'm going to bear country."

"Don't move away, man. You gotta stay here till I save you."

"Okay, no problem."

Pete returned to his mother. It wasn't the same now, Florian saw. Lenore was arranging daycare for Pete, filling Chub's old time slot. And Chub didn't fight it, even helping by staying away from the building. But when they saw him at Kelly's, bending over his accustomed pool table, his game seemed to suffer. Even McGonigle noticed and seemed touched, pulling Chub to the bar to buy him a drink. He felt the need to explain himself, though, since he'd proclaimed Chub a boob.

"Any man what bleeds a pint or two," he said, "I ain't above puttin' the pints back in."

Chub laughed and Florian turned to the mirror to see them all frontally. He noticed himself apart from his companions, from their emotions of the moment, but it didn't bother him. The others were patching things up, a rare sign of progress for the old building on Basil Street.

4

The crowd in Lenehan's had declined by the time the story ended, most of the patrons now mourners from Edward's wake. Florian and I had had enough to drink and so decided to brave the elements. The cold air outside was bracing, both of us expressing wistful pleasure as we walked to my car. I'd offered to drop Florian at his hotel and he'd gratefully accepted.

"Can I give you a lift to the funeral tomorrow?" I asked in the car.

"Well, it's the whole shebang, you know. Mass and then a cavalcade to the cemetery, et cetera. You're up to all that?"

"Sure, why not? There'll never be another Edward."

"Hm. Well, let's hope the weather holds up."

I glanced over at him to share the joke, but he was looking straight ahead, his mouth a straight line. I attended to the driving.

The funeral Mass was indeed a drawn-out affair, with assorted eulogies by relatives of Edward and some of his countless associates and friends. The gathering in the church was smaller than I expected, considering the crowd at the wake. The procession to the cemetery traveled quite a distance through midday traffic. There was a long-established family plot, it developed, around which we stood in a merciless raw wind. The interment was hastened along and the mourners invited to complimentary lunch at a nearby restaurant. I drove the short distance with Florian, finding that the place doubled as a garden center during warm weather, with cemetery flowers available year-round. The parking lot was surprisingly full considering the location and modest nature of the restaurant. The reason, we quickly learned, was that many of our fellow mourners and drinkers from the wake had skipped the Mass and interment and proceeded directly to the lunch. They were already spread across the main room, liquor flowing and heads wagging, the occasional horse laugh thrown out.

"Maybe we can join the locals in the wings," I suggested.

"Retain a modicum of dignity," nodded Florian.

We sat as far from the din as we could, near a window through which we saw snow starting to flurry. We settled in cozily with drinks and light meals.

"This is a life-saver," I said, glancing toward the main room. "That makes two in as many days."

Florian smiled, then dropped his gaze to the table, thoughtful.

"But there's a greater feat than saving a life, of course."

I waited him out, only frowning a bit in curiosity.

"It would be saving a soul. I think we'd agree it's much rarer, though our reasoning might well be different. Not that many souls aren't lost, however you think of the soul, but how often is an outsider, one with a separate soul, able to decisively save the soul of another?"

"I sense a story coming," I said, and I was right.

5

At the very front of the courtyard building, on the middle floor, lived an elderly lady who left her plants on the sills. As building manager, Florian worried about this. Should one of the pots fall on a passerby, he might be held responsible and lose his job. Combined with his flimsy work history, it could be devastating to his future prospects. So he saw it as necessary to approach Miss Nubbe and appeal to her better judgment.

"They can fall," he said. "The owner would be liable."

"But that's a public sidewalk. The city would be liable."

"No, because the pot would be leaving private property, your window sill, and striking someone before it reached public ground."

"What about public airspace?"

He was standing in it himself, looking up as Miss Nubbe did her watering. The red and orange flowers were taunting, it seemed, while the purple were seductive.

"It doesn't matter," he said. "We'd still be liable. Can't you just keep them inside?"

"Oh, but Florian. We've been setting them out for ages. Since you were a boy, I imagine. I could change myself, of course, but what about Maddy? Changes upset her, Florian. You wouldn't want to hurt her, would you? Send her off before her time?"

Madeline, her sister, lived in a mental twilight. She spent entire days in a living room chair while Miss Nubbe puttered about.

"Maybe you could prepare her—for the pots being inside, I mean. But you do see the problem, Miss Nubbe—don't you?"

She continued the watering, attending to the flowers at the expense of his question.

"You know," she said, "I'll have to ask a favor of you, Florian. Do you think you can stay with Maddy tonight? I really must be getting to confession."

They still had it nightly at St. Vincent's, two blocks away. She knew he'd been a monk, of course, so she thought he'd see the importance. And as monk and manager, she could trust him with Maddy. She figured she had his number, Florian thought, and she was right. But it was only because of the plants, his need for her to cooperate with him.

"There's no one else?" he asked.

"Not on a week night. Not since we lost Aloysius, rest his soul."

She'd mentioned him before, an alcoholic brother twenty-four years in his grave. The flowers that were kept had apparently been his favorites. Once Aloysius was mentioned, Florian's moral stand was weakened. He could recover, it seemed, by doing the dead brother's job. Then he'd have leverage in the movement of the pots.

"I'll stay with Maddy," he said.

Miss Nubbe stopped watering and smiled at him, her wreath of white curls like an evening cloud.

"Thank you, Florian," she said. "I'll pray for you with my penance."

The sun had set when he returned, and the plants were in for the night. Maddy was still in her chair, looking vacantly about, and Miss Nubbe was quickly on her way.

"Mustn't be late," she said. "Father Duffy starts right on time. And as soon as there's no one on the kneeler, it's back to the rectory with him."

Alone with Maddy, Florian felt entombed. The sister was wrapped in a bulky robe with a black scarf around her head. Her pale, putty-like face was expressionless, her hands lying on the armchair as if she'd forgotten about them. The light was dim, the sisters pinching pennies with low-wattage bulbs.

"Is that you, Aloysius?" asked Maddy.

"No, it's Florian. The building manager."

"Not in limbo, then? Still around are you?"

"Your sister asked me to stay with you. She's gone to confession over at the church."

"Confession? At the church? You've been to the priest then, Aloysius? Praises be, you're off the bottle then! Yes, you're off it and—praises to Mary and Elizabeth—you're back with us, brother! Alive and well and sober and hard-working! And for a decent wage, if you please. What a day this is! What a fine and glorious day!"

"No," said Florian. "You must understand. I'm not Aloysius."

"Not Aloysius, are you? You'll try me with that, brother? Oh, always the jokester you were, spinning your tales at the pub and bringing us limericks from those wags. Putting us on at every turn, you were. Though I gather that'll be changing now, Allie, you being purged and all. Though it wasn't purgatory you was in owing to it not being your fault. Still, you can't pass through limbo without learning something, can you?"

"I just came here from my apartment, one of the efficiencies at the back—"

Maddy laughed, her head tilting back.

"Yes, I know about that! Sary's old place, where you'd go and play dominoes with her. Though Sis and me used to wonder, Allie, if your hands was really on those pieces. Maybe *Sary* was your domino, I'd say."

She laughed again, higher and longer, staring into Florian's face. But she seemed to be looking through him, he thought, seeing someone at a greater distance. When he glanced over his shoulder, of course, no one was there.

"All right, Maddy," he said, "just relax. We'll have a good, long talk about the old days."

The pasty old face was pleased. Aloysius was pardoned for his foibles, the fault not being his, while blame was heaped on a nineteenth-century Pa.

"A mean one he was," said Maddy. "Beat you bloody before the age of reason. No wonder you took to drink and the rest. Limbo was the only place for you, Allie. But don't worry. We'll be getting you out of there soon. Sis is working on it. So she says, anyway, and Sissy's word is good as gold. You know that, now—don't you?"

"Oh, yes," said Florian. "Yes, I know. But tell me, Maddy, what exactly is Sis doing? Does it have to do with the flowers there?"

"Heavens no, brother. That wouldn't spring a ladybug. No, Sissy's making the book of prayers. You must have seen them go by, floating through limbo to the Maker. That's quite an account building up, I'd say. Won't be long now, Allie."

"Until the release from limbo?"

"Right you are, brother. Then you'll be all atoned for and ready to wait in heaven for Sis and me. And don't think we mind none of this, Allie. We know it was family what abused you so it's family what needs to get you out. And Sis is working on it, all right. Won't be long."

"What about yourself, Maddy? Do you say any prayers?"

"Do I—? Aloysius, you wag, you know you used to kid me about living on my knees. But that's no more than gossamer next to the book of prayers. Has to be in writing, brother, to register upstairs. And that's Sissy's cup of tea, now. Can't lend a hand myself. Arthritis. I try to keep her at it, of course, but she's a bit touchy at times. Age, you know. But then I guess you wouldn't, leaving us prematurely like you did."

Florian humored her, awaiting Miss Nubbe's return. On the saner sister's arrival, he left immediately, feeling he'd well earned the sills without flower pots. When he checked the next day, however, he saw they were back out again, one with its bottom extending over the edge.

"Miss Nubbe!" he called.

When she came to the window he could see she was anxious. Her mouth was a tense "oh" and she was wringing her withered hands. Her appearance made him hesitate, unsure whether he should complain just now.

"Oh, Florian," she said, "heaven must have sent you! Excuse my foolishness, but it's *urgent* that I get a sitter for Maddy tonight."

"Tonight? What's the problem, Miss Nubbe?"

"Time is running out and there's something I need to finish. Something important, Florian, extremely so. I have to receive guidance for it from Father Duffy. Please, could you stay with Maddy again like you did last night?"

"You're going to confession again?"

"Yes."

"But surely you couldn't have sinned much since last night."

"Oh, that isn't the point, Florian. A great sin *will* be committed if—well, I simply *must* get to Father Duffy!"

"Can't Maddy go with you?"

Miss Nubbe glanced behind her, then held a finger to her lips.

"Maddy never goes *anywhere*," she said. "It's too hurtful to her. She watches the Mass on television and that's the only show we watch. The rest are too upsetting for her."

Florian gave in. He meant to get those pots inside and had already invested an evening. He didn't want to blow everything now. He'd make his pitch again when Miss Nubbe calmed down. Besides, he thought, maybe her seeing the priest would make her more reasonable. Maybe the priest would steer her right.

6

Maddy wasn't surprised that evening when Florian arrived.

"Ah," she said, "there you are, Aloysius."

"Yes," replied Florian. "I just made a visit to the bathroom."

Maddy smiled, her eyes appearing tired.

"I was thinking while you was in there," she said, "about the times we had. Pa was a bad one, of course—a chum for the devil now, no doubt. But the trips we took on the streetcar, Allie, with Ma—remember those? Watching the buildings slip by—the banks, the finely dressed people. All the way uptown we'd go, eat at the dime store counter without Pa staring at us—you spilling mustard without getting the clout in your ear. And we'd walk along the waterfront, and window-shop, and go in the city library to see the domes on the ceiling. And it was all of a sunny day, with the flowers in the window boxes. Even then you liked the orange ones, Allie."

She smiled on him and Florian felt queasy. Impersonation, like all dishonesty, wasn't within his repertoire. He was still a monk that way.

"Why did you have to take to drinking?" Maddy asked.

Her tone was plaintive, more a grievance than a question.

"Well," said Florian, "surely you must know."

Maddy looked away from him, her face crumpling.

"Ah yes," she said, "surely I do."

"But that's all past now, Maddy. It can't be helped. What matters now is the future, gathering your strengths, your abilities, to—"

"Ah sure, the future! Blessed be Joseph and Mary, and remember we Ruth and Esther, the Good Samaritan, and Father Damien! The book of prayers, brother—that is what matters now. And I got after her, I did, while you was in the jakes there. She'll be working on it, she will! We'll have you sprung from limbo well afore the whistle, never fear."

"The whistle?"

"When time's up, brother. The twenty-five years since we laid you to rest. And well earned it was. But we pledged a prayer a day recorded in the book, a proper record what to present for springing you. Sissy was doing it faithful but she left off. Had an admirer for a time but that's all done now. And I couldn't do nothing myself, Allie, being as how I was. So it was behind we were, more and more, and now the race is on to get the prayers recorded. Don't worry though, brother. Sis will take care of it. I know that in my heart. In my mind, too—the temple of the Holy Spirit!"

She nodded emphatically. Florian looked around, wondering where the book was kept. Not that he wanted to see it. Intruding on anyone's prayers was opposed to his training. But he wondered how far Miss Nubbe had to go. She was apparently having trouble with her commitment, then running off to Father Duffy and dumping Maddy on himself.

He went by her window the next day, hoping to talk with her away from Maddy. The flower pots were out but he tried to ignore them. He thought he was ready but, as soon as Miss Nubbe appeared, she was already talking.

"I can't leave Maddy now. Come again this evening, same time. Goodbye, Florian."

"But, Miss Nubbe—"

"Extremely urgent! Come at the same time!"

And she was gone. The sky was overcast and Florian wondered anew why the plants had to be out. But there was no reasoning here, he thought. He looked down Basil Street toward Wexler, the market on an opposite corner. That was the way she'd go tonight. He felt like going that way himself, giving Father Duffy a piece of his mind.

But instead he made a phone call, explaining things in a collegial manner.

Florian returned to Maddy again, while Miss Nubbe bustled off to Father Duffy. As if she'd read Florian's thoughts, Maddy revealed a crusty old album that was the celebrated book of prayers.

"Here it is, Aloysius—your ticket to eternal joy."

She was beaming, ardently believing in the tattered old book's supernatural qualities. In the dim light of the apartment and the eerie aspect of Maddy, Florian almost believed her.

"Don't touch it now," she said. "It might be spoiled if there's limbo prints on it."

She turned the first few pages, which were brown with age and chipping at the edges. The ink of their entries had faded so they were barely visible.

When Maddy flipped to later years, the entries were shorter and written in bunches. There seemed, however, to be a minimum length of eight to ten lines.

"Beautiful, ain't it? And she's just got this much to do, brother."

Florian's jaw dropped. It was at least a fifth of the book, maybe a quarter. Five to seven years of entries, with daily trips to Father Duffy for forgiveness. The priest must have known about this, Florian guessed. How could he possibly have thought he could handle it?

When Florian passed beneath the window next day, he heard a repetitive punching sound from the sisters' apartment. Since the pots were out as usual, he called Miss Nubbe. She didn't appear. The punching continued and Florian called again, more loudly. The window was suddenly filled with Maddy, her bulky robe like a mountainside.

"Aloysius!" she said. "They let you out in the daytime now! Sis, come see! It's Aloysius in the daytime! All saints be praised!"

Miss Nubbe didn't come and the punching kept up. A sense of alarm swept over Florian. He hesitated a moment, absorbing Maddy's intensity, then rushed into the courtyard. He was quickly inside, up the steps, hammering on the sisters' door.

"Maddy, open up! I have to get in!"

No response, but he realized that the punching had stopped. Then, slowly, the door was unlocked and opened. Miss Nubbe stood before him.

"Whatever's the matter, Florian?"

"I—I heard a sound. And Maddy—well, she was acting different."

"Things *are* different now, Florian. All our problems are solved! Yours too, I dare say. No more need for you to stay with Maddy, and I'll bake you a nice pie to show our appreciation. What flavor do you like, Florian?"

"What? Oh, rhubarb will do."

"I'm not sure that's in season. Do you have a second choice?"

"Miss Nubbe, I'm a bit confused. How did—I mean, what did Father Duffy say to you last night? Of a practical nature, I mean."

"Oh, he was *very* practical, Florian. He gave me something he'd gotten from his young assistant, a spiritual tool he called it. I'm using it to finish the book on time. Aloysius will be free!"

She was trembling with excitement. Maddy towered behind her, a fixed smile on her face.

"That punching sound," said Florian. "Was that the tool I heard?"

Miss Nubbe laughed.

"Punching? Oh, Florian! Come and see for yourself!"

He entered the apartment, following the women to a table where the old book was opened. Florian saw at once that the latest entries were in purple, neatly rectangular, and in printing. Moving closer, he saw that the prayers were identical.

"I have fought a good fight," each said. "I have finished the race, I have kept the faith. Finally, there is laid up for me the crown of righteousness, which the Lord, the righteous Judge, will give to me on that Day, and not to me only but also to all who have loved His appearing."

Near the book was an open stamp pad. On it was the rubber stamp, handle glistening, the vital tool for Miss Nubbe's labors.

"The assistant used it with the school teams," said Miss Nubbe. "He stamped it on their gym shoes and they'd say it before the games."

"He'll be wanting it back, then."

"No, Father Duffy said to keep it. I don't think he altogether approved of the shoe-stamping. As a matter of fact, Florian, I was thinking of giving it to *you* when I'm through. A keepsake, you know. You *are* a religious, more or less, and it'll hold you till I make the pie."

Florian grunted. What he'd do with the stamper he didn't know. Pass it along as a gift, perhaps? Well, he was glad to be through with Maddy so he gratefully accepted the spiritual tool. He wasn't quite through with Miss Nubbe herself, though. She continued to put out the flower pots, even when Aloysius was out of limbo. He could see them better from heaven that way, she said.

7

    Our wing of the restaurant was near empty by story's ending, but many of Edward's raucous mourners still lingered in the main room. We'd had a second round of drinks but, not being lifted to the level of the early arrivals, we avoided them on leaving. The wind outside was still biting but the flurries seemed harmless to driving. We'd agreed that I'd take Florian to the train station, and I planned to see him off as friends still sometimes do. Traffic was light and we reached the downtown area in plenty of time. Leaving an expensive parking lot, we entered the huge station and took an escalator down to the old waiting room with its ticket windows.

    "You had a round-trip ticket?" I asked Florian.

    "Yep. One-way from a monastery doesn't look so good."

    We stood for a moment in the cavernous space, absorbing the echoes of steps on the tile floor, suitcases slammed about, voices.

    "I see the Iron Horse is still in business," I said with a nod toward the bar.

    "Do they still call it that?"

    "It's a while till your train. Shall we?"

    Florian moved in the bar's direction.

    "Ah, the inevitable point of reconnaissance on past and future."

    The place was sparsely populated due to the early hour. We stayed at the bar itself and had a couple of sips in silence, Florian more subdued than usual.

    "And so you depart," I ventured.

    "Yes. Yes, I do."

    "It sometimes seems life is a string of departures, though that should mean a string of entrances, too, don't you think?"

    "Well, yes, assuming—" He hesitated.

    "There's something on the other side?"

    He only smiled and leaned on the bar, gazed into the mirror behind the bottles.

"I'm reminded of when I left the apartment building, working my way back to the monastery. I didn't return directly, you see."

"Do I correctly sense a story coming?"

"Not this time, James. My ticket is time sensitive. Just an idea about entrances, as we were saying. As if you don't have to leave and arrive, die and be reborn, to be transformed. There might be portals along the way that—well, contain wonders."

I listened for more.

"You remember Hardball?"

"The one who got you the building manager job?"

"Steered me to it, yes. He'd left the city before me, taken this job in a remote area. It was some kind of animal husbandry project, might have involved cloning. It was all pretty secret. Hardball was working as a guard, armed, sometimes in a tower. He had a cabin in which I stayed a few days on my visit. He'd gotten close to this daughter of the owner, or manager, of the project, so I guess I was kind of in the way from her point of view."

"Three being a crowd."

"Yes, more or less. Anyway, Hardball took me into the woods one day to show me something he'd found there. This was a cold day with snow on the ground. After a pretty good hike we spotted a pinkish cloud in a clearing. There was a warm pool beneath it, surrounded by light brown boulders. The Bay of Beige, he called it. It was fed from underneath, apparently, and ten feet down would make you red."

"He bathed in it?"

"Yes, and so did the girl, Mandy. Hardball invited me to try it but I shied away. Monkish modesty, you know, plus the fact that it was winter. But then something happened—"

Florian hesitated. I waited, not wanting to alter his recollection.

"I was up early one day, getting some coffee going, when Mandy came to the door looking for Hardball. I told her he wasn't back from his night watch, and she went away. But then I decided I should tell him about her coming. I went to the watchtower but found no one there. There were footprints leading off to the woods, so I followed them in a ways until I strayed from the trail and heard noises to one side. It was Hardball, running back from the Bay of Beige, and he was nude."

"This was part of the bathing routine?"

"Yes, and—" Florian smiled wryly. "Not just for him."

"The girl?"

My companion nodded.

"Saw her the next day. I was up early again, thinking about things, when I saw the flash coming out of the forest. She headed for the watchtower, really moving. I hung back and she didn't see me. I didn't bring it up with Hardball but he seemed to have an inkling I knew. He even mentioned I could still try the Bay of Beige if I wanted to. And I was tempted, delayed my departure for a day or two. I didn't think they'd go again so soon but, as I watched in the next pre-dawn, I saw Mandy headed for the watchtower. And I prepared to go myself."

"To the pool in the forest. Nude bathing. With the others? Both of them?"

"I watched from the bushes as they clasped each other, rose up a bit, then dipped beneath the surface with force. They came up with greater force, propelled by something unseen. When they separated and were treading water amid the steam, I suddenly realized how cold I was and made a mad rush on the pool. I yelled something and jumped up off the boulders, landing with a splash that showered over them."

"How did they respond?"

"Hardball was fine, laughing in fact, but Mandy was appalled. She made a few comments until Hardball calmed her down. The funny thing is, she *really* calmed down. The effect of the pool, maybe. It even transpired that—on Hardball's suggestion, urging—she and I took that dive together. Down into the force of the pool. And the feeling was fantastic. Clasping her as we dove, then shot back up, it seemed we were ready for anything!"

I tried to envision the situation, Florian at its center.

"Well. A moment away from monkhood."

"Yes, I'm afraid so. But you know, James, it was also a baptism for me, crude as the analogy may seem. I was more ready to return to the monastery, as if I'd gained a layer of understanding, eased the pain of what I'd been dealing with. I could see potential in the unknown, a balance for the sordidness of the known."

"An epiphany for you."

"Yes, if you will. An epiphany."

"So then you left them? Hardball and Mandy?"

"Yes, it was just the one dip. They had their relationship, after all, and I'd had my time at the portal, sampled the wonders it held. I was ready to sing hymns again."

I stared into my glass.

"I never envied you before, Florian. But I must say, that one experience—"

"I know, I know. Words can never describe."

It was too close to departure to have another drink, so we finished up and left the bar. Florian bought a newspaper to read on the train and we continued to the concrete piers. It seemed we'd exhausted our store of conversation and sentiments, so we simply shook hands to mark another parting.

"Goodbye," he said. "Say a Hail Mary for me."

"Yes, I'll do that."

Boarding the train, he leaned back and flashed an ironic smile.

"Epiphany!" he said, and was gone.

I kept my promise back at the station bar, silently reciting the words over a cool stein and packet of nuts. I hadn't noticed earlier how the bottles before the mirror, in the reflected colored lights, resembled saints at a celestial opera.